DARKNESS GROWS

AFTER THE EMP BOOK TWO

HARLEY TATE

DARKNESS GROWS

A POST-APOCALYPTIC SURVIVAL THRILLER

Four days into the apocalypse, would you still be alive?

The day the power went out, Madison gave up her college-student life and risked everything to make it home to her mom in Sacramento. Tracy fought off looters and thieves to prepare for her daughter's return. Now reunited, they must defend themselves from everyone else.

What would you do to see your family again?

Walter watched the lights blink out across the country from 37,000 feet up in the air. Emergency landing a 747 in the middle of nowhere turned out to be the easy part. With riots and fires creating chaos, finding his way home might get him killed.

The end of the world brings out the best and worst in all of us.

With the power grid destroyed and the government unable to help, the Sloanes find themselves stuck in a city growing increasingly desperate. Will Madison and Tracy have what it takes to survive with neighbors and thieves closing in? Can Walter make it home to his wife and daughter before disaster strikes?

The EMP is only the beginning.

Darkness Grows is book two in *After the EMP*, a post-apocalyptic thriller series following the Sloane family and their friends as they attempt to survive after a geomagnetic storm destroys the nation's power grid.

Subscribe to Harley's newsletter and receive an exclusive companion short story, *Darkness Falls*, absolutely free.

www.harleytate.com/subscribe

DAY FOUR

SIXTY HOURS WITHOUT POWER

CHAPTER ONE

MADISON

Sloane Residence
Sacramento, CA
7:00 a.m.

I WILL NEVER TAKE COTTON SHEETS AND A GOOD MATTRESS for granted again. Madison stretched her arms over her head and rolled over. The sky outside hung in the liminal moment between dark and light, sunrise still a few minutes away.

If Madison hadn't been up at dawn most mornings in college, she would never know such a space existed. The handful of minutes before the sun spilled over the horizon had always signaled the start of something new for her. Hope, anticipation, the promise of more.

But three days ago, everything changed. How long

would it take for the world to notice? How long could her friends and family survive?

The geomagnetic storm that hit the earth didn't discriminate. The EMP destroyed every inch of the power grid it touched. How many people were powerless? The West Coast? The entire country? Continent? World?

Without a means of communication, Madison didn't know. But that wouldn't stop her. Whether the government or the military or relief charities showed up wouldn't be the difference between her survival or her death. *No.* Madison would survive, and she would keep her friends and family alive, too.

After one last stretch, she swung her legs over the side of her bed, narrowly missing Peyton's head on the floor. Her best friend from college might only be a calendar year older, but he more than made up for it in height and width.

Peyton's arms stretched from the edge of Madison's bed all the way to the door on the other side. His head poked out of his sleeping bag like the sack had been made for a child. If she didn't know him so well, she would assume he played on the UC Davis football team as a proud Aggie. Instead, he spent his days by her side in a stuffy greenhouse watering tomato plants.

Easing her feet down between his sleeping bag and her bed, Madison sneaked around Peyton and out her bedroom door. The tiny two-bedroom bungalow her parents called home wasn't made for six people, but no one seemed to mind.

They had a roof over their heads and enough food

and water for weeks thanks to her mom's quick thinking. Madison grabbed the portable radio off the hall table and poked her head in the living room, pausing as her eyes adjusted to the light.

The bright yellow sleeping bag on the floor reminded Madison of a butterfly cocoon, bumpy and lumpy with a still-sleeping form inside. But the sleeping bag next to it was gone. Madison smiled. *Tucker must be awake.*

She found him a few minutes later, crouched in the backyard, tinkering with something on the ground.

"Whatcha doin?"

He turned, brushing a clump of shaggy black hair out of his eye. "Trying to rig this solar panel to charge my laptop. You?"

"Wiping sleep from my eyes and jonesing for a hot cup of coffee."

"Better watch out, too much caffeine will stunt your growth."

Madison put her hand up as if to guess at her own height. "Now you tell me." She walked forward with a grin and joined Tucker on the edge of the patio. A three-section piece of canvas sat unfolded on the ground, the blue solar panels on top waiting for the sun.

She motioned at it. "You really think you can power your laptop with that?"

Tucker nodded. "I've done it before just for fun. It might take a day or two, but give it enough hours of solid daylight and it'll charge."

Leave it to an astrophysics major to know how to keep technology going even without the grid. Madison chewed on her lip. If the solar panel could charge Tucker's laptop battery, what else could it do? "Any chance that could run a coffee pot?"

Tucker laughed. "Not unless you've got a spare power bank with a 120 volt receptacle lying around. I looked for one when we were loading up on supplies, but the store was out of stock."

Madison sighed. "It was worth a shot." She stood up and clicked the radio on, turning the dial in slow-motion, hoping for anything other than static. No luck. Shouldn't the government be saying something by now? Doing something?

The sliding door to the patio opened and Brianna, Madison's roommate from college, stood in the open doorway, eyebrows scrunched together.

"How long do you think before that crazy guy comes back and wants all our stuff?"

"Good morning to you, too."

Brianna pressed her lips together. "Sorry. I'm cranky without coffee."

"Me too." Madison stood up. "I don't think Bill is coming back any time soon. After my mom threatened to shoot him, he backed down pretty quick."

"He pointed a shotgun at you, Madison."

Madison corrected her. "Bill pointed a shotgun at all of us."

"That doesn't make it any better." Brianna stepped onto the patio and walked over to Tucker. He wrapped an arm around her shoulder and gave her a squeeze before letting go.

She didn't want to admit it, but Brianna had a point.

The man had shown himself to be a hothead who didn't take no for an answer. Add in the fact that he'd seen some of their supplies in the back of Brianna's Jeep and Madison knew Bill would be trouble.

Part of her wished they could just batten down the hatches and pretend the rest of the world didn't exist. Inside her parents' house, they were safe, secure, and could survive. Unfortunately the rest of the neighborhood knew it, too.

How many neighbors would side with Bill? How many would come knocking on their door demanding a share of their food and water?

Madison thought back to the neighborhood meeting only the day before. It seemed like months ago, not hours. She still couldn't believe how unprepared and naïve everyone appeared.

Did most of the population believe the power would come back on? Did they really think this was no different than a bad thunderstorm and downed power lines?

Madison ran a hand through her hair, tugging at the tangles in the brown strands. It had been long enough since she'd showered that her hair had passed the greasy stage and entered disgusting.

She wondered about all the homes tucked into her parents' neighborhood. What were the occupants doing right now? Would they be allies or threats? With a glance back at the open sliding glass door, she asked the question out loud. "How many houses are in the neighborhood, do you think? A hundred? More?"

Brianna scratched at a spot behind her ear.

"Probably a hundred and fifty. Maybe two hundred. We drove by a lot of places on the way in. Why?"

"There were about thirty people at the neighborhood meeting yesterday, right?"

"I counted thirty-three." Tucker stood up before continuing. "But some of those were from the same household. I met a few married couples. "

Madison nodded. She might have gone through hell the last three days to get from Davis to Sacramento, but people had stayed home. Most people still didn't know.

She perched on the patio table as she thought it over. "Let's assume there's at least a hundred houses around us that didn't attend. That means there are a hundred houses who didn't hear Tucker's explanation for the power loss. They don't know about the EMP."

Glancing at Brianna, Madison dropped her voice to ensure it didn't carry past the small backyard. "That's a hundred families in this neighborhood alone who are sitting in front of their televisions, checking their phones, and waiting for the power to come back on."

"I still don't get what you're saying." Brianna crossed her arms, her pink plaid shirt a stark contrast to the T-shirt and camouflage cargo pants she had worn the last few days.

Madison focused on the lines parading up and down the flannel. "I think we're still ahead of the game. We're some of the few people around who know what's happened."

At last, Brianna nodded in understanding. Her father had been a survivalist for as long as Madison knew them, fortifying a cabin up in the mountains for just this situation. "As long as we have the upper hand, we should take advantage."

"You mean we should go on a run." Peyton walked outside, the orange cat her mom had saved the day before tucked into his arm. Fireball mewled and Peyton let him go, watching as the cat greeted each person with a headbutt and rub across the legs.

"Maybe?" Truth be told, Madison didn't have a plan, but every minute that ticked by without them shoring up their defenses and gathering more supplies was a minute wasted.

She reached down and scratched Fireball's head behind the ears and the little cat meowed his appreciation. "I know we have a lot, more than most people, but…"

"Someone will try to take it." Brianna held out her hand, ticking each finger as she ran through a list. "We have food. Water. Shelter. That only leaves one critical item: weapons."

"We have a shotgun and a pistol." Peyton frowned. "Add in Wanda's gun and that's more than enough."

Brianna snorted. "It's not anywhere close. But that's not the real issue. We could have an entire arsenal full of guns but they won't be any more useful than a sack of rocks if we don't have any ammo to go in them."

Madison nodded. She wished they could all just stay home, but they couldn't. "Brianna's right. Bill knows we have food and water. He saw Wanda's gun since my mom pointed it at him. If things get ugly around here, he won't leave us alone. The sooner we can defend ourselves the better."

Peyton crossed his arms. "It's too dangerous, Madison. We could get ourselves killed."

"We did just fine at the mini-mart."

"That was luck. What if the shop owner hadn't run out the back? What if one of those thugs hadn't died in there? One of us could be lying facedown between the Twinkies and the Snickers, rotting in a pool of our own blood."

Brianna wiggled her nose. "Thanks for that mental image."

"I'm serious." Peyton glanced at Tucker. "Help me out, man. You can't want your girlfriend going back out there."

Tucker pushed his hair off his face. "I don't. But she's right. At some point the two of us are heading to Truckee. Brianna's parents need to know she's okay. We can't leave without a way to defend ourselves and if we take a gun from here, you won't have enough."

Brianna joined in. "We have, what, a partial magazine of rounds for the handgun and a box of shells for the shotgun? It's pathetic."

Peyton opened his mouth to argue again when a chipper voice interrupted.

"Who wants grilled pie for breakfast?" Madison's mom Tracy stepped onto the patio, a tray full of baking supplies and fresh apples in her hands. She stilled as she caught sight of all their faces. The tray wobbled in her hands. "What's going on? Did something happen?"

Madison exhaled. Her mom might have stuck a gun in Bill's face the day before, but that had been to protect her only daughter. Madison didn't know how she would react to her plan.

"We've been talking about the future. What we need to do to prepare."

Tracy raised an eyebrow. "Prepare for what?"

"The people who will come to take what we have. The ones like Bill Donovan. You know he won't be the last."

Her mom frowned. "I was hoping we could ignore that for a day or two."

Madison managed a small smile. "Me, too. But we can't. Now is the best time to go out there."

Brianna nodded in encouragement and Madison took a deep breath. "Don't freak out, but we need more guns and ammunition. We're going on a supply run."

CHAPTER TWO

TRACY

Sloane Residence
    8:00 a.m.

"Over my dead body." Tracy palmed her hips. Madison might have survived a harrowing drive from her college campus to home, but that didn't change the fact that she was nineteen and barely an adult. "No daughter of mine is becoming an arms runner four days into the apocalypse."

Peyton stifled a laugh.

At least someone agreed with her. Tracy softened her stance. "I know you mean well, Madison, but it's dangerous out there. People are... horrible." She glanced back at the inside of the house.

Her former boss still slept inside, tucked into a pile of blankets on the couch. If she hadn't picked Wanda up at the bus stop, if they hadn't gone back to Wanda's apartment on the very same type of scouting mission Madison now proposed…

Visions of the two thieves they had encountered filled her mind. The one with greasy hair. The other holding a six-pack of beer and the keys to a car she so desperately needed.

Tracy steeled herself. Madison might think of herself as tough, but in the moment, would she have the strength required? Would she be able to look a man in the eye and take his life? Tracy would never forget the way the first man she shot looked down at his chest, watching in horror as his own blood coated his shirt.

She had done what she had to in order to protect Wanda and herself. But she couldn't ask her daughter to do the same. Killing a person wasn't something you could take back or get over. It would haunt Tracy forever.

"Mom, we'll be fine."

"No." She shook her head. "I just got you back. I won't risk losing you again. If anyone is going on a weapons run, it's me."

"But Mom!"

Tracy smiled at her daughter and picked up the tray of food. "Enough about this for the moment. Who wants breakfast?"

9:30 A.M.

11

IF ONLY WE COULD PRETEND FOR A FEW HOURS LONGER. Tracy leaned back in her chair, a cup of instant coffee in her hands. After talking her daughter off the gun and ammo ledge, Tracy had convinced the four college kids to huddle around the patio table and learn how to make hand pies to grill in the backyard.

Peyton's continuously growling stomach didn't hurt, either. The boy had to eat five all by himself.

But now they sat staring at empty plates, Wanda included, waiting for something to happen. Anticipation hung in the air around them like an early Sacramento fog. The more Tracy thought about Madison's comments, the more she agreed with them.

Regardless of who stayed in the house and who left, they would need more ammunition—a lot more. A few more shotguns, a knife or two, and some pocket pepper spray would all come in handy. But where would they get it?

And who would go?

She glanced at each member of her new household. Tucker, the physics geek, seemed responsible and sensible, but he was still a twenty-year-old young man. Brianna, Madison's roommate and Tucker's girlfriend, was as gung-ho about survival as anyone Tracy had ever met. But that didn't make her a good choice.

Peyton hated the whole idea and wished everyone would stay home and barricade themselves in. And Wanda...

Despite showing a bit of resolve in her apartment, Wanda couldn't be trusted with much more than her own person. Tracy knew she was a liability, but she couldn't ask her to leave. She hoped the longer she stayed, the more she could grow.

Survival took more than ingenuity and skill; it took resolve.

At last, Tracy settled her gaze on her daughter. Madison was deep in conversation with Peyton, arguing the finer points of container gardening in the Sacramento heat—something they would need to perfect in the coming months.

She couldn't ask any of them to come with her. Singling someone out would be tantamount to declaring him or her expendable. Tracy couldn't do it. Oh, how she wished Walter were home. Just the thought of her husband's name shot a pain through her heart.

He could be anywhere from Hong Kong to the Sacramento airport right now. When he'd left the morning of the geomagnetic storm, he had kissed her goodbye just like it was any other day. If only they had known a few hours earlier... If only someone had warned them...

Tracy exhaled. Walter was the strongest, most dependable man she knew. She had to believe in him. No matter how long it took, he would make it home; Tracy knew it.

"All right." She sat forward in her seat and reached out to take the empty plates. "We should come up with a plan. I'll need two volunteers to come with me and three to stay behind. There's a Walmart about five miles from here. If anywhere still has ammunition, that'll be the place."

Brianna stood up. "I'm coming with you. I'm the

only one who knows what ammo we need just by looking at the box."

Tracy nodded. "Who else?"

"I'll come." Tucker stood up and joined his girlfriend. "If Brianna's going, I should come too. We're the ones who will probably leave first, so it makes sense for us to scope out the area, see what kind of activity we'll encounter on the road."

She had to admit their reasons made sense. Tracy glanced at her daughter. "Is that all right?"

Madison frowned. "It was my idea. I feel like I should go."

Brianna shook her head. "No. Your mom's right. Someone needs to stay behind. I don't trust that Bill guy. He might come back and besides me, you're the only one who knows how to shoot."

Madison stared at her roommate for a minute before nodding. "Okay. But at the first sign of trouble, you all need to come home."

Tracy smiled. She would make it a point of thanking Brianna and Tucker for being so brave and selfless when they hit the road.

With a deep breath, she stood and began collecting the plates. "Let's all get ready. Madison, you and Peyton need to set up a watch schedule. Someone should be monitoring the street at all times."

Madison and Peyton nodded.

"Wanda, can you clean up the house and update the supply list I made a few days ago? We'll need to start using the garbage bags I bought. I don't think the trash will be picked up this week."

Tucker snorted his agreement. "Just think about how bad the cities are going to smell soon."

"Ugh." Brianna made a face. "What I'm wondering is how we go about setting up a shower."

Wanda surprised Tracy by speaking up. "When I was little, we had an outdoor shower to clean off before coming inside. It was gravity-fed. I might be able to recreate it."

Wow. Maybe Wanda would be an asset after all. "Thank you." Tracy smiled at her former boss before turning to Brianna and Tucker. "As for the two of you, let's get ready to go. There's one place we need to stop before the Walmart. I made a promise a few days ago and I need to honor it."

CHAPTER THREE

WALTER

TEN MILES SOUTH OF THE CALIFORNIA-OREGON Border

10:00 a.m.

"A BLUE RASPBERRY SLURPEE. FOUR-DOLLAR FROZEN coffee with some name I can't pronounce. The ice cream shop where they mix in M&Ms on top of a cold hunk of marble." Drew leaned back in the passenger seat, groaning as he exhaled. "That's just the cold stuff."

Walter shook his head. "Why do you want to torture yourself? Just be thankful for what we do have."

Even without looking, Walter could feel the death-ray stare. "Speak for yourself, but driving a tin can for a car down some backwoods road halfway to nowhere isn't my idea of a good time."

"It's not?" Walter laughed. "Funny. I took you for the mountain-man type."

Drew flipped down the visor and scoped out his three-day-old beard in the mirror. "Really? You think I can pull off the lumberjack thing? Anne always wanted me to grow a beard. Said I'd be the hippest pilot flying out of Sacramento."

"I was joking."

"Oh." Drew flipped the visor back up and resumed his slouch.

Walter's co-pilot Drew Jenkins had progressed from denial, to horror, to resignation all in the span of a few days. Witnessing the end of the modern world from 37,000 feet up in the air could do that to a person, Walter supposed. When the crash landing didn't jolt Drew out of his fog, Walter had hoped the altercation outside the bank in Eugene, Oregon would have taken care of it.

But no. If anything, Drew had slid into an even more precarious state. Instead of rising up and defending his own life when someone threatened it, he stood on the sidelines and let Walter take the lead. Walter might be in the best shape of his life, but forty-seven-year-old muscles and bones weren't half as good as a thirty-year-old's. If Drew didn't grow a pair, and soon, the man wouldn't make it in this new world.

"Next shop we see, we're pulling over. I need some caffeine and something more to eat than a Clif Bar."

Walter scrubbed at his face. "Mr. Harbin was generous to give us what he did. We could have left with nothing." After emergency landing a 747 on a tiny airstrip outside of Eugene, Oregon, Walter didn't know what to expect. Thankfully, they'd landed at a private airfield and the owner, George Harbin, had been more than welcoming.

Drew straightened up in the seat. "That doesn't mean I don't want a damn Twinkie."

Walter kept the retort on the tip of his tongue to himself. He wasn't happy about their circumstances, either. A canceled flight and a quick drive home to his wife would have changed everything. But life didn't always work out the way a person wanted it.

No sense in dwelling on it.

They would make it home to Sacramento. He would reunite with his wife, Tracy, and find their daughter. Every minute that ticked by was a minute longer his family was alone in a city growing increasingly unsafe. How long could they survive on their own?

How long before someone tried to take what wasn't theirs? How long before Tracy's strength was tested in ways she never imagined?

Walter tightened his grip on the steering wheel and eyed the gas gauge. An eighth of a tank. He sighed. They needed gas, and soon. "How far do you think we are from Sacramento?"

Drew yawned as he thought it over. "We crossed into California, what, ten or fifteen miles ago?"

Walter nodded. They had both almost missed the little wood sign on the side of the road. A pine tree had grown in front of it, obscuring the words, Welcome to California. A far cry from the multilane divided highway most people used. But if the traffic jam outside of Eugene was typical, then all of I-5 was bumper-to-bumper.

The highway might as well be an unlit fuse cutting through a puddle of gasoline. All those people stuck on the road, running out of gas and food while the sun beat down. A spark would set the whole highway ablaze with fights and riots and destruction.

They might be taking the scenic route, but at least they were alone. For now.

"If we don't run into a gas station soon, we'll be walking the rest of the way."

Drew leaned over and scoped out the gauge. "An eighth of a tank? I thought these little things were supposed to drive forever on one fill-up."

"We idled on the highway for hours not going anywhere. It ate a lot of gas."

"Shit."

"Exactly."

The two men rode on in silence, intermittently checking the gas gauge and scoping out the rural, wooded scenery passing them by. The low fuel light came on.

No gas station in sight.

The car dinged and beeped, warning them of their dire fuel situation.

Still just picturesque forests and dappled sunlight.

Walter glanced at his watch. Based on their speed, he figured at least another hundred and fifty miles to home, if not more. He couldn't be sure where this road led or what they would encounter. The car sputtered, engine seizing on the last bits of gasoline.

He scanned the horizon. Trees. Blue sky. Nature at its finest.

Any other day, he'd be thrilled to be out there, off the grid, breathing clean air, listening to birds and squirrels in the brush.

Not today.

The car coasted to a stop, engine dying as the last drops of fuel ran dry.

Drew cursed and looked out the window. "We can find a car. Siphon it."

"Have you seen one in the last hundred miles?"

"No. But there has to be someone out here somewhere. A house, a shop, something. We can't be that far from civilization."

Walter exhaled and reached for his bag in the back seat. "Say we do find a car, what then? Do you have a spare tube in your duffel? A container to put the gas in? A way to get it back in our car?"

With every question, Drew slouched further in his seat, a frown turning his boyish features into a petulant child's face. "No."

"Then face it. We're walking." Walter pushed open the driver's side door and got out, stretching his arms high above his head. The car might not get them anywhere fast, but it still had utility.

He bent down to catch Drew's attention. "Quit moping and get out here and help me. We aren't leaving anything useful behind."

Drew clambered out as Walter popped the trunk. "What are you talking about? All we've got are our overnight bags and dress shoes."

Walter's eyebrows rose. "If that's all you think we

have in the car to use, you're even more hopeless than I thought. Didn't you do Boy Scouts or go camping as a kid?"

Drew shook his head. "Nope. City born and raised. If I can't buy it or pay to have it done, I'm a bit hopeless I'm afraid."

"Then prepare yourself, Drew. I'm about to teach you a few things." Walter all of a sudden felt very old. When he'd retired from the Marine Corps as a lieutenant colonel, he'd felt his age. All those nineteen- and twenty-year-olds looking up to him like he was their grandpa, calling him the Old Man.

But once he'd returned to civilian life, forties were the new twenties. He'd never felt so young. Now, for once, he was thankful for his experience. Being the old guy had some advantages.

He reached down and lifted the fabric liner of the trunk, exposing the spare tire and its tools. The tire iron came out with a tug and Walter handed it to Drew.

"What am I supposed to do with this?"

"Beat someone over the head with it, if need be. It's a weapon, Drew. A damn fine one."

His co-pilot stared at the tire iron in his hand like it was an alien life form.

Walter didn't have time to ease Drew into the apocalypse. He would either figure it out or die trying. Scoping out the rest of the trunk, Walter grabbed a rubber band holding the spare tire instructions together and the cargo netting still wrapped in factory plastic.

Then he moved onto the interior. With a well-aimed

tire iron to the overhead lights, Walter broke the plastic casing and retrieved the light bulbs, setting them on the seat before checking the glove box for anything useful. A paper clip. *Excellent.*

He motioned to the rear seat. "See if you can pull the seat covers off. We can use the foam underneath. If there's any cotton batting, let's grab that as well."

"Have you turned into a hoarder? What do we need all this crap for?"

"You'll thank me when the sun sets." Without another word, Walter went back to work, pulling the wires from inside the cigarette lighter and fishing around for anything else that might be useful. Paper receipts, a wayward pack of gum with foil wrappers, a half-empty water bottle he discovered lodged under the driver's seat.

After wrapping the light bulbs up in his clothes and stuffing the rest of the items in his duffel, Walter helped Drew finish stripping the rear seat. *Jackpot.* A thin layer of batting separated two layers of foam core. Walter rolled it up and stuffed it in his bag before joining forces with Drew to pull out the foam.

After tugging on it for a few minutes with no success, Drew stepped back. "Before I break out into a sweat, will you tell me what the hell we're doing?"

Walter bit back a smile and motioned at the foam. "How comfortable do you want to be on the ground tonight?"

Drew blinked. "We're going to sleep on it?"

"Unless you'd rather just rough it."

Drew regarded him for a moment before bending

back down and giving the foam another tug. "Let's strip the front seats, too."

After another hour or so of scavenging and packing, they were ready. Walter hoisted his bag, now lashed with rolled-up car foam and seat covers, over his head. He glanced at the sky. "We've got about three hours of daylight left. Let's make the most of it."

CHAPTER FOUR

WALTER

FOREST OF NORTHERN CALIFORNIA
6:00 p.m.

"THIS LOOKS AS GOOD A PLACE AS ANY. I SAY we stop."

Walter checked his watch. "How about another half hour? We can get another mile or two before sunset."

Drew grimaced and pointed at his feet. "Dress shoes aren't made for hiking. If we go too much farther today, I'll have hamburger for feet."

Walter understood the pain of blisters and bleeding skin. He might have been a pilot, but he still trained like every other officer in the Marine Corps. Substitute deciduous forests for the pines and redwoods surrounding them and Northern California wasn't that different from Quantico.

He motioned at the road in front of them. "Let's

clear this hill. There should be a good vantage point around this bend and then we can decide."

Drew grumbled under his breath, but kept walking, his steps awkward from the rubbing of his shoes. As they crested the hill, Walter hushed him.

"Look."

A roofline sat barely visible among the trees, the brown of its metal roof blending with the forest all around.

Drew squinted and stuck his neck out, peering into the distance. "At what? All I see is miles of forest."

Walter pointed at the peak of the roof again. "There's a cabin just through there. About two hundred yards off the road."

At last, Drew spotted it. He turned to Walter with a frown. "What do we do?"

Truth be told, Walter didn't know. "We could see if anyone is home."

Drew shook his head. "We're in the middle of nowhere. You really think whoever took the time to build a house way out here wants visitors?" He glanced around at the never-ending trees. "People don't come out here because they want to socialize."

"It could be abandoned." Walter cinched his bag higher up his shoulder. "It would give us shelter for the night. Maybe a few supplies."

He knew walking up to the front door of a cabin a handful of days into the end of the world wasn't the best plan, but what other options did they have? They could keep hiking with barely any food and water left, no real means to keep warm at night other than scavenging to start a fire, and no weapons besides a tire iron and Walter's wits.

Or, they could scope out the place, do a little reconnaissance, and possibly earn a good night's sleep out of the elements. He thought about Tracy and Madison and the pair of them spending another night wondering if he would ever come home. Where was his daughter right now? Did she make it home already? Would he need to set off to find her when he reached Sacramento?

Walter opened up his duffel bag and checked the contents. One more bottle of water and a granola bar. That was it. Drew couldn't have much more. With as many as a hundred and fifty miles to go before they reached home, they wouldn't make it.

Not without more provisions.

He zipped the bag shut and exhaled. "We need to check it out. If you want to stay here, that's fine. But I'm going in."

"You're serious?" Drew's eyes went wide, but the set of Walter's jaw must have told the man all he needed to know. After a moment, he composed himself. "All right. But I'm going with you."

"Suit yourself." Walter began the descent down the hill toward the cabin's concealed driveway. "When we reach the road in, we'll drop our bags, scope it out, and come back to get them if it's clear."

"And if it's not?"

Walter smiled, but it wasn't from humor. "We run like hell and hope we don't get shot."

"Comforting."

"Nothing about the current state of the world is comforting, Drew." *It might never be again.* Walter stepped ahead of his co-pilot, hugging the edge of the road with each step. The broken asphalt crunched beneath the soles of his shoes and Walter focused on the sound. They were hundreds of yards away from the place, but the noise concerned him.

Walking up to a stranger's cabin in the middle of the Northern California woods might be crazy, but he didn't have a choice. Without water, food, and shelter, they would never make it home. They needed to get off the road.

At last, a weed-covered drive broke the tree line into two and Walter slowed, raising his hand to stop Drew behind him. The duffel slipped from his shoulder and Walter eased it onto the ground.

His voice barely reached a whisper. "We can stash the bags in this ditch and approach from the side."

Drew set his bag next to Walter's in the depression next to the road and followed him into the forest. "What should I do?"

Not get shot. Walter exhaled. He knew Drew was only looking for some reassurance. A little training would up his confidence, maybe even make him an asset instead of a liability. Walter thought back to his land navigation training. It had been more years than he cared to admit since Walter had needed foot-patrol skills, but he still remembered the key signals.

"Ready for a crash course?"

Drew nodded.

"First, keep a few steps behind me. Never get too

close. Next, if I raise my hand in a fist like this," Walter bent his arm at ninety degrees, fist straight up, "it means freeze."

"Okay."

"If I swing my arm up quickly with my palm open, it means come forward." He demonstrated the motion until Drew nodded.

"You'll be ahead of me, so what if you see someone or there's a threat?"

"It's the reverse of the forward signal. If you need to take cover, I'll raise my arm and then drop it quickly. If I do that, get on the ground or hide behind a tree."

Drew's brow knitted. "All right. Can you run through those again?"

Walter demonstrated each signal a few more times until Drew seemed confident. He could tell the man was running the motions through his head over and over, trying to memorize them.

A two-minute course in silent patrol wasn't easy for a civilian, but Drew was right—walking into a potential hostile situation without a means to communicate was a fool's errand.

As they prepared to set off, Drew spoke up. "What means run like hell?"

Walter managed to keep his smirk in check. "The sound of gunfire should do the trick."

Drew paled. "You think someone will shoot at us?"

Walter turned back to the forest. "Plan for the worst. Then you'll always be prepared." He raised his arm, palm open, signaling for Drew to come forward. With the sun setting any minute, they needed to get on with it.

CHAPTER FIVE

TRACY

Sacramento, CA
11:00 a.m.

JOE TRAVERS LIVED IN A TINY RANCH LESS THAN A mile from the library Tracy used to work at five days a week. She couldn't believe how much had changed in such a short time.

"How did you say you know this guy again?"

Tracy glanced over at Brianna with a smile. "He was a regular at the library. Always looking for a new thriller author to read." Her sunny expression faltered. "If it weren't for Joe, we might not be having this conversation."

She focused on the road with a frown, willing back the tears that threatened to fill her eyes. Joe's explanation of the effects of solar weather had been the reason Tracy loaded up on supplies. If it hadn't been for him… She cleared her throat. "Solar weather was his hobby. He's the one who explained Coronal Mass Ejections and EMPs to me."

Tucker leaned forward from the back seat. "If he knew about it, why are we checking on him? Shouldn't he be prepared?"

Tracy inhaled through her nose and exhaled through her mouth, barely able to keep her voice steady. "Joe is in his eighties and walks with a cane. Even if he knew about the EMP potential, he wouldn't have been able to do much."

Brianna and Tucker fell silent. She didn't have to explain that four days without power could be the difference between life and death for a person that age. They didn't need to see the bodies in the retirement community where Wanda lived or talk to the manager there to confirm it.

She just hoped they weren't too late. The little Nissan Leaf cruised silently down the street, the battery powering the vehicle at low speeds. Tracy didn't know how long the little car would last, but so far, so good.

As long as they kept their drives to a minimum, they might be able to rely on the car for a few weeks. Tracy glanced at the houses as they drove down residential streets—every one still mowed and maintained like the power outage was a blip on an otherwise ordinary week. All the husbands and wives were probably standing in front of their picture windows surveying their domains, thinking *surely it will come back on tomorrow*.

She snorted to herself. *Not happening*.

As they turned a corner a person caught her eye.

The woman couldn't have been much older than herself, blonde hair pulled back in a haphazard ponytail. Skintight athletic pants hugged toned legs. A tank top showed off arms tanned by the Northern California sun.

From a cursory glance, she looked like any other woman in the neighborhood. But as Tracy slowed the car, other tells became apparent. The dark circles under her eyes. The grease shining her hair more than usual. The hollow look to her cheeks.

She looked tired. Hungry, even.

Tracy turned back to the road, her grip tightening on the steering wheel. Was this the future? In a month would that woman even be alive?

Glancing at the two teenagers with her on this trip, Tracy frowned. Brianna with her golden curls and Tucker with his bright eyes and pale skin. They might have plenty back home, but other people would be hungry soon, if they weren't already.

Most people Tracy knew only had a few days' worth of food. Tiny houses meant tiny pantries. People relied on the corner grocery store or the nearest fast food restaurant instead of their own supply.

If all of the houses they drove by were almost out of food, what would happen in the coming days? If FEMA or a local charity didn't show up soon...

Tracy shook off the spiraling thoughts. She could only control her own actions, no one else's. As she turned the corner, she pointed down the street.

"Joe's house is just ahead."

Slowing the vehicle, Tracy scanned the mailboxes for Joe's number: 126, 128, 130... 132. *There.* A tidy little white house with black shutters and a red door. Old school, just like Joe.

She pulled into the drive and killed the engine. "Are you two ready?"

Tucker glanced at his girlfriend before nodding. "I'll stand watch outside."

Tracy climbed out of the car with both kids right behind. Unlike so many houses they passed on the drive over, Joe's front lawn sprouted with weeds. Fluffy white heads of dandelions waved in the breeze and blooming clover buzzed with honeybees. The place looked unkempt. Abandoned.

Maybe that's his plan. A vacant house wouldn't have anything worth stealing. It wasn't a bad strategy, all things considered. Tracy made her way to the front door and pulled open the screen. Her knock sounded hollow as it echoed through the house.

Brianna shifted beside her, fidgeting with a lock of hair as Tracy knocked again. "Joe? Joe Travers? Are you in there? It's Tracy from the library. Just came to check on you."

Tracy cupped her hand around her ear and pressed her head to the door, listening. Nothing. Not a single sound besides her own breathing. The red door reminded her of her grandmother's house. She only visited the woman once or twice.

The first time, Tracy had been so full of hope. Grandmothers were supposed to care. They were supposed to be plump, bouncy ladies with fresh-baked muffins and lots of kisses. The woman whose bony hand

Tracy shook didn't have a kind bone in her body, much less the humanity required for a kiss.

The second time, Tracy knew better. No one would save her. No one in the little white house with the same red door would take her in. She stepped back with a frown. She had a feeling they couldn't save Joe, either.

"I'm walking around back."

Brianna nodded, her teeth nibbling on her lower lip like a mouse with a piece of cheese. "Don't take too long. This place is giving me the heebie-jeebies."

Tracy stepped into the weedy grass, peering in every window she passed, but seeing nothing. The mini blinds kept the outside light out and her peering eyes from glimpsing the inside. A short chain-link fence separated the front from the back and Tracy opened the gate, pushing it just wide enough to slip through.

She scanned her surroundings. A worn privacy fence. Scraggly bushes. Small concrete patio with a county trash can and recycling bin. Nothing out of the ordinary.

The back door appeared as solid as the front and closed up tight. Tracy tried the door handle, but it didn't budge. She bent to the ground and fished beneath the mat. He had to keep a spare key somewhere.

After five minutes of fruitless searching, Tracy palmed her hips in frustration. She wasn't leaving without getting inside. Best case scenario, Joe had packed up and left for greener pastures. Worst case, he was sucking in his last breath as she stood outside, fretting over what to do.

"Any luck?"

Brianna's voice startled her and she jumped.

"Sorry."

"It's okay. I was looking for a key, but I can't find one. I'll have to break a window."

"You sure you want to do that? What if he's just out for a drive?"

"Joe doesn't drive. His license was revoked last year."

"Oh." Brianna pointed at the window by the back door. "That's probably your best bet."

The window stood just higher than hip level, with a single pane in an aluminum frame. Tracy stepped closer and peered in. Single crank to open it, no screen to speak of. It looked original to the house, which meant it wasn't tempered. When she broke it, the glass would shatter in nasty, jagged pieces.

Tracy wished she had some tape or a blanket; anything to muffle the sound. But they didn't think that far ahead and they were running out of time. This was only the first stop of the day. Walmart was next.

She turned around and surveyed the yard. A brick from the landscaping edging would have to do. After digging it out of the ground, Tracy hoisted it up. "If you see or hear anyone, come get me. Otherwise, wait out here."

"You sure?"

Tracy nodded. "I won't be long." With a deep breath, she pulled back and launched the brick at the window. The glass shattered and the brick took the metal mini-blinds with it, clattering to the floor along with massive shards of glass.

Great. So much for being quiet.

Tracy knocked the remaining glass from the bottom of the window and after tossing her jacket over the sill, she hoisted herself up. It was a tight fit, but she made it, slipping into the dark house and landing on a pile of glass. It crunched beneath her feet, drowning out the rapid beating of her heart.

"Joe? Joe are you here?"

Tracy stood in the dark kitchen, blinking until her eyes adjusted to the dim light. As the room came into focus, she frowned. Stacks of cans sat on the kitchen table, alongside boxes of shelf-stable milk and pasta. A few kitchen cabinet doors stood ajar, revealing tidy stacks of plates and glasses, but no food.

Had Joe been preparing to leave? Did something happen? She called for him again, but heard no response. She would need to go room by room, searching. She exhaled. *Here we go.*

The kitchen opened into a small living room and breakfast nook, both neat and empty. Off the living room, a hallway led to the two bedrooms and single bath. Tracy braced herself. If Joe was still there, she hoped he was still alive. Please be sleeping. Or too sick to stand.

She could handle that.

Tracy reached for the first door handle, turning as she pushed the door open. An office. She exhaled in relief. She opened the next door and found a small bathroom with a pedestal sink, toilet, and tub/shower combination. That left only one door. The bedroom.

Before she opened the door, she knew. On some level, she'd known since the very first day. Saying goodbye to Joe that fateful day when the world changed… She knew, but she wasn't prepared.

Tracy pushed the door open and her hand flew to her mouth, half because of the stench and half because of the sight. Joe lay in bed, hands on his chest, his skin gray from death. She walked around the edge of the bed, shoes silent on the plush rug, and stopped at his bedside table.

An empty bottle of nitroglycerin tablets stood beside a water glass, and a piece of paper sat beneath them. Tracy blinked. It couldn't be.

She pulled the piece of paper out from beneath the glass and bottle and gasped. It was a letter addressed to her.

Dear Tracy,

I hope this letter finds you well. If you are standing beside my bed reading this, then take comfort in the fact that you have survived. From the moment I met you four years ago, I knew you were one of the good ones.

A person with more kindness in her than fear. A woman with an open heart and a backbone of steel.

When the power grid failed, I knew my time had come to an end. An old man who can't walk more than a quarter mile without a rest can't survive in a world without electricity.

Instead of leaving at the wrong end of a gun or after days of no food and water, I've chosen the quick and painless way out.

Before you leave, please take the food I've stacked in the kitchen. There are also a handful of supplies in the office, along with a twelve-gauge shotgun and a box of shells. She hasn't been fired in years, but she's a dependable old gal, so you can rely on her.

The coming days and weeks will test you like you've never been tested, but you will find a way. You are a survivor. Remember that.

Take care of your daughter. She'll need you to show her the way.

Until we meet again,

Joe Travers

P.S. Ignore that science fiction book sitting on my desk. I'll always be a thriller fan at heart.

TRACY WIPED AT HER EYES BEFORE HER TEARS RUINED the last words from Joe she would ever read. What a good man. He had not only warned her of what was coming, but he made sure her trip to his house wasn't in vain.

She looked down at his peaceful form. How she

wished she could bury him. But they didn't have the time. It would take hours to dig a deep enough grave. If someone caught them…

No. Joe wouldn't want her to risk it. As much as she hated it, Joe was in his final resting place. She leaned over and placed a kiss on his cold, wrinkled hand.

Thank you for everything.

Half an hour later, she unlocked the back door and walked out with a shotgun hanging off a strap on her shoulder and a cardboard box full of food in her arms.

Brianna stood up, brushing off the dust and dirt from the concrete patio. Her eyes bounced between the gun, the box, and Tracy's puffy face. "Is he—"

Tracy nodded. "Took his own life."

"I'm sorry, Mrs. Sloane."

"So am I." She hoisted the box a bit higher and motioned toward the front yard. "Let's get on the road. I'm done here."

Following Brianna back out to the driveway, Tracy said a final goodbye to Joe. She needed to put this morning behind her. They were on a mission.

CHAPTER SIX

TRACY

Walmart, Sacramento, CA
1:00 p.m.

Seven. They had only passed seven working cars during the entire drive across town to Walmart and four times as many abandoned on the side of the road. Tracy didn't know what it meant. Was everyone else still stuck on the highways? Had most cars run out of gas already? Were most people staying home?

She pulled into the parking lot of the super center, wary and on edge. If the place had already been ransacked, who knew what unsavory types still lurked inside. On the other hand, if no one had broken in, would their attempts trigger a backup alarm? Would the police show up?

Tracy hadn't seen a single police officer since the power went out, but Madison had relayed their run-in with a local cop. They couldn't be arrested. Madison and the others needed them.

"I don't see any activity." Tucker sat twisted in the back seat, scanning the lot and building. "We should go around back."

"Why?" Brianna frowned at her boyfriend. "The front doors aren't locked down. The metal grate is wide open. I say we just ram a cart through them and go on in."

"Tucker's right. We need to keep a low profile. If anyone's in there, breaking through the front doors is a surefire way to let them know we're here."

Brianna crossed her arms. "The back door won't be any better. Aren't they usually metal?"

Tucker leaned forward, arms braced on the front seats. "I worked the stockroom last summer at the one in Davis. The loading dock will be the best place to break in. Half the time the rolling garage doors aren't even locked."

"Really?" Tracy found such a lack of security surprising.

"Most of the big Walmarts accept deliveries twenty-four hours a day. Why pay for a lock when the loading door is always open?"

If anyone knew about saving money, it was Walmart. Tracy followed Tucker's suggestion and drove around the warehouse to the loading docks. She backed the Leaf into the bay against the far wall and shut it off.

"All right. We need a plan." She turned to face the two college students. They were so young. Part of her hated putting them in danger. But she didn't have a choice. She needed more eyes and ears and hands than her own.

"I say we split up. We'll cover more aisles and be able to grab more supplies."

Brianna glanced at the loading bay door. "That's assuming we can even get in."

Tracy nodded. "First, we check the doors. If there's one that's open, we go in, shut it behind us. We can spend the next few minutes scoping out the store. If it's secure, we can split up. I'll take camping and automotive. Brianna, you head for guns and ammo. Tucker, can you handle food and water?"

"You betcha." Tucker rubbed his palms together. "If we run into trouble, what should we do?"

Tracy managed a small smile. "Scream as loud as you can and run like hell."

Brianna let out a short laugh. "I like your style, Mrs. Sloane."

"Call me Tracy, please."

Brianna's eyes lit up. "Okay, Tracy. After you."

Tracy opened the driver's side door and stepped out. Brianna and Tucker followed a moment later. They climbed up onto the loading bay and Tucker reached for the handle.

"Here goes nothing." He tugged and tugged and tugged. "Guess this one's locked. I'll try another."

On the sixth door he let out a whoop. "It's open! Come on." Tucker pulled the rolling bay door up just enough for them to duck underneath. As soon as they are inside, he slid it shut. They were cocooned in darkness.

Tracy stood still, listening. "Do you all hear anything?"

"No. And I can't even see my fingers."

Tucker flicked on a small flashlight. "The whole place is gonna be pretty dark. We'll have to use flashlights."

Tracy nodded. She didn't like the idea of broadcasting their locations to anyone else in the store, but what choice did they have? She clicked hers on. "You two stay here while I go check out the warehouse floor. Don't move unless you hear me shout."

Before either one could argue, Tracy set off, flashlight beam bouncing across the linoleum as she made her way to the main floor entrance. She flicked the light off as she neared the door.

Please let no one be here. Please.

After a deep breath, Tracy inched the door open.

No noise. No light. *Thank goodness.*

She scanned the warehouse three times before turning and calling for Brianna and Tucker. "It's clear. Let's go."

Two flashlight beams appeared and in moments, the kids were by her side.

"There should be carts just outside the door. I say we each grab one and load it up."

"Good idea." Tracy led the way and sure enough, Tucker was right about the carts. She pulled three out of the stacked line. "All right. We meet back here in thirty minutes."

Tracy watched the light beams of Brianna and Tucker's flashlights disappear in different directions

42

before heading for the far corner of the store. The front left cart wheel wobbled on every revolution, causing the cart to shimmy for a moment. Tracy concentrated on keeping it headed straight as she walked down the dark aisles.

With every step, she passed another example of American consumerism. Comforters. Dishes. Kids' ride-on toys. Microwaves. Tracy snorted at that one. Half the store would be worthless now: all the electronics that would never turn on, movies that would never be watched, CDs never to be listened to again.

A display of car windshield wipers caught her eye and Tracy turned the cart down the aisle. Halfway down, she found what she was looking for. Gas cans. Bright red plastic cans sat one after another in neat rows, biggest on the bottom, smallest on the top. Tracy grabbed two large and two medium and placed them in her cart.

To the left hung siphon pumps and spigots and Tracy grabbed one of each. Without working gas pumps, they would need to siphon gas soon. On down the aisle and Tracy piled the cart full of cans of instant fix-a-flat, a rooftop cargo carrier, and other random car supplies.

In the next aisle, she paused, eyes wide as she stared at the racks stuffed with car batteries. For the first time since leaving the house she thought of Walter. Her husband would know which batteries went with which type of car and whether they could use them for anything else.

She thought back to her physics classes so many

years ago. A battery could light a fire, power small electrics…hell if it could start a car, it could do a million other things. Without another delay, Tracy loaded the bottom of the cart with as many batteries as would fit. They might not get a chance to come back.

After exhausting automotive, Tracy hit the fishing section, grabbing poles and tackle boxes and an assortment of bait and lures. They could drive to Folsom Lake and fish if they had to. She'd taken Madison there as a kid. It wouldn't be fished clean for a while.

Then there was the tiny survival section with everything from commando saws to paracord bundles to stormproof matches and water filtration. Tracy piled it all in the cart until small items were tumbling off the sides.

A week ago and Tracy would have been shocked at her own behavior. This was theft, plain and simple. But what did it matter? Four days without power and not a word from the government. Not a single broadcast over the radio or knock on her front door.

Joe was right. life as they knew it was over. No one would be coming to help. Tracy shined the flashlight down the aisle before turning the cart around. Like a lumbering beast with too heavy of a load, it groaned beneath the weight of supplies.

As she gave it another push, Tracy cocked her head. *What was that?* A wave of apprehension shivered through her. *Was that a voice?*

Tracy clicked off her flashlight and snuck behind the end cap, leaving her cart in the middle of the aisle. She couldn't be more than five aisles from Brianna, sporting goods the only category between camping and ammunition.

Creeping on silent feet, Tracy worked that way, feeling with her hands in front of her for the next end cap. She strained to listen past the quiet and hear once more the noise that raised the hair on her arms.

There.

A voice. She was certain. Man or woman, she couldn't tell. They were either all the way across the store or whispering nearby.

Five. Four. Three. Two. One.

Counting backward did little to stem the rising thud of her heart inside her chest. The terror, now too familiar, of strangers. Visions of the burglars from Wanda's apartment complex filled her mind. She still doubted her decision.

Pulling the trigger—killing those men—seemed like the only way out. But what if she was wrong? What if she had acted too fast and taken a life too soon? Was her humanity already hanging by a thread?

Would the thin line connecting Tracy to her old life snap in the middle of a dark Walmart, her cart full of stolen goods stashed a few aisles back?

With shaky fingers, Tracy wiped a grimy sheen of sweat off her brow before forcing her lungs to fill with air. The shotgun from Joe's apartment suddenly felt like a lead weight slung over her shoulder, a grim reminder of the future and her part in it.

She wouldn't become someone else. Not today. They had enough supplies back home to last a while. Finding Brianna and Tucker and getting out before anyone spotted them was key. The stuff she had collected could stay behind.

Tracy eased around the corner, the faint light from the front of the store filtering in a straight shot down the next aisle, lighting up the silhouettes of two people fifty feet away. One look at the wide stance and broad shoulders of each person and Tracy knew she had found a pair of strangers.

She just hoped they made it out before the interlopers found them.

CHAPTER SEVEN

WALTER

FOREST OF NORTHERN CALIFORNIA
7:00 p.m.

THE SUN SET TOO DAMN FAST AROUND HERE. WITH the tree cover, Walter couldn't see more than five feet in front of his face. It seemed every step he took, the trees crept closer, obscuring his sight and forcing him and Drew too close to the clearing.

He eased beyond the last layer of trees and held up his hand in a fist. He didn't know if Drew could even see him at this point, but he had to try. If anyone was going to brave walking up to a cabin weaponless and exposed, it would be him. Drew would get himself shot before he took five steps.

With night coming on fast, Walter didn't waste time assessing the perimeter or watching from a safe distance away. He guessed the useable light, or what passed for it at the moment, would only last another few minutes.

Standing with the forest to his back he made the only sensible choice. He strode toward the cabin, head held high, body relaxed. In eight paces he reached the front steps, planting his feet one after another until he stood in front of the door.

His heavy knock echoed through the woods.

"What are you doing?" Drew's hissed question came from the dark just beyond the porch.

"What does it look like?" Walter knocked again. "I'm seeing if anyone is home."

Drew's head appeared around the side of the building, a darker round mass barely distinguishable from the emptiness beyond. "Whoever's inside could shoot you."

"If they wanted to, I'd be dead already. We both would be." Walter took a step back and cupped his hands around his mouth. "Hello? Is anyone home? We're stranded and need some help. Hello?"

"I thought we were supposed to be all stealthy and crap. Not barge right up and shout." Drew climbed the stairs at last, stopping beside Walter. "Why teach me hand signals if we're just going to knock on the front door?"

Walter exhaled. "I didn't realize how dark it would get, or how quickly. It's been a while since I've been out in the woods." He moved toward the window beside the door, stopping when his forehead almost brushed the glass. "We lost any ability to scope the place out when we lost the light. Walking up to the front door was the only other option."

They weren't on a covert mission with night vision goggles and flak jackets and M-16s with ACOG scopes. For all the training Walter possessed, he was also a middle-aged man with tired feet, aching muscles, and the need for a night's rest. Not that he would tell Drew any of that.

His co-pilot fidgeted beside him, bouncing back and forth on his feet as he glanced at the dark surrounding them and then back at the cabin. "I don't think anyone's home."

Walter crouched down in front of the mat. "Probably not." He ran his fingers under the edge, searching. When he came up empty, he stood and did the same with the top of the door frame and the windows, but still nothing. He frowned. There had to be a spare key somewhere.

"Can you walk up the driveway to grab our stuff? I'll find a way in."

"Why don't you just break the window?"

"Have a little respect, man. Someone owns this place."

Drew scoffed. "You didn't care about the rental car. You stripped that thing to the metal rivets holding it all together. Why the sudden conscience?"

Walter turned to face Drew. He couldn't see more than his shadow in the dark. "My conscience has been here the whole time. The rental car ran out of gas. It's no good to anyone in the middle of nowhere with no gas in it. The rental car company is never going to be in business again."

Drew began to interrupt, but Walter spoke over him. "This place is someone's home. It might be a vacation spot or a survival cabin or the main place someone lives. But regardless, it might be the only thing standing between the owner and death. I'm not going to ruin that."

"Seems to me survival is an all or nothing enterprise, Walt. Either we are or we aren't. Picking and choosing who we steal from and who we hurt doesn't make much sense."

Walter ran his hand down his face. "I haven't abandoned my moral compass because the power is out, Drew. I still give a damn about my fellow man."

His co-pilot snorted. "Tell that to the thugs we left behind in Eugene."

"They were trying to steal from us!"

"How are we any different?" Drew turned, a shadow blending into the night, and walked down the porch steps. "I'll go get the bags, but if you haven't found a way in by the time I get back, I'm breaking a window."

Walter stood there, staring as Drew walked up the middle of the dirt and gravel driveway, his receding figure a contrast to the pale ground beneath his feet. Was Drew right? Were they no better than those two men who demanded everything they had?

No. They weren't the same. Walter had defended himself from an obvious predator then. He wasn't the aggressor in that situation; it was the man whose windpipe he crushed who attacked first.

Walter only had better skills and a hard punch.

He shook off his doubt. The world was changing from civilized to wild. When he attacked those men in Eugene, he knew they wouldn't give up without a show of force. But the cabin he stood in front of wasn't a man out to rob him. It was shelter and rest. Recovery and a chance to plan.

Taking his time and respecting the owner was the least he could do. Until humanity and common decency became liabilities one hundred percent of the time, Walter would use his best judgment. Today, they still applied.

Placing his palms beneath the window frame, Walter pushed, hoping it wasn't locked, but the window didn't budge. *Damn it.* There had to be an easy way in somehow.

He strode around the side of the cabin, assessing the options. Another window sat high on the side and Walter didn't waste any time. With his hands gripped on the rough log wall, fingers digging into the grooves for purchase, he hauled himself up. Two feet off the ground and he could test the window.

The groaning sound of wood on wood as it moved might as well have been the opening chord of Walter's favorite song. With a few more shoves, the window opened enough for him to fit inside.

Using the sill as leverage, Walter hoisted himself up and shoved his upper body through the gap. The smell of wood and dust hit his nostrils, confirming no one was home. The place must not have been aired out in months.

He dragged the rest of his body through and landed in a heap on the wood floor. A cloud of dust bloomed around him and Walter covered his mouth to keep from sucking in a lungful.

As he stood, Drew's voice sounded from the front. "Are you in yet or do I need to find a rock?"

Walter hustled up to the front door, banging into a coffee table and almost knocking over a chair on the way. "I found a way in. Hold on."

He managed to unlock the door and swung it wide.

His duffel hit him smack in the chest. "Good, because these bags are heavy and I need a break."

Drew eased past him and flopped on the single couch, sending another cloud of dust into the air. His hacking cough made Walter smile.

"I forgot to tell you the place needed a good cleaning. Sorry."

"No you're not." Drew chuckled as he stretched out and kicked his shoes off. "Damn, this feels good."

Walter bent to fish his flashlight from his bag and turned it on before shutting and locking the cabin door. "Don't get too comfortable until we check the place out. If we need to leave in a hurry, we should be ready."

Drew groaned. "Speak for yourself, but I'm not going anywhere. The place would have to be on fire, flooding, and under attack before you could peel me off this lumpy couch."

Walter smiled. "You were pretty quick to run back in Eugene."

"That's before I walked five hundred miles." Drew leaned back and launched into song, his voice cracking and off-key as he belted out the lyrics to "I'm Gonna Be."

"Good thing we aren't hunting tonight. You've probably scared off everything from rabbits to feral cats with that screeching."

Drew sang even louder when he hit the part about waking up next to a woman and Walter thought about his wife.

Tracy needed him. Madison, his daughter, needed him. Part of him wanted to push on, to not stop until he fell at the doorstep of their house in Sacramento.

But what good would that do? How could he help them exhausted and hungry? He needed his wits and strength to be an asset. As Drew kept on singing, Walter surveyed the cabin. They weren't five hundred miles from home, but they still had a few days' worth of walking ahead.

His flashlight beam bounced over a dry sink and cabinets, a table for two with turned legs and faded black paint, and a cot nestled in the far corner. The place wasn't much, but it was warm and dry.

A lantern on the counter caught his eye and Walter reached for it. A small butane fuel cartridge ran the light and he shook it with a smile. One flick of the switch and a couple pumps of the starter and the cabin turned from a black hole to a dim glow.

Things were looking up. One night there and they would come up with a plan. They didn't have a choice.

Walter walked over to the cabinets and tugged open the first one. His eyes lit up in surprise. *We've come to the right place.*

CHAPTER EIGHT

MADISON

Sloane Residence
8:00 p.m.

"Where are they? They should have been home hours ago." Madison paced in the kitchen, fingers twining around each other as she fidgeted and worried. *I never should have let them leave without me.*

With one hand, she tugged her hair back off her face and looped it into a loose bun. It was still damp from the shower Wanda managed to rig up in the backyard. Who knew a five-gallon bucket and some old plastic tubing could be so handy?

But even the soap and water didn't wash away Madison's worry. Her mother, Brianna, and Tucker wouldn't be out after dark unless something happened. She knew it.

"Your mom said they had to stop somewhere first, right? Maybe it took longer than they thought."

Madison paused long enough to cast a glance at Peyton. "You think so?"

"It's as good a theory as any." He ran a hand towel over his wet hair to rub it dry. "I don't know how clean I am after using the same water you all did to shower, but at least I got wet."

"Even dirty water gets the stink off."

"Does it?" Peyton lifted his arm to smell his armpit. He scowled. "If you say so. But deodorant works a hell of a lot better."

Madison stopped to peer out the front window for the fiftieth time since she wandered into the living room. "What if one of them is hurt? What if they ran into someone else? What if other people already broke into Walmart? They might need our help."

Peyton perched on the arm of the sofa. "Your mom asked us to stay here. She wouldn't have done that if it wasn't important."

Madison crossed her arms. "She did that to keep me safe."

"That's not the only reason." Peyton motioned to the baseball bat sitting by the front door. "Don't forget about our visitor the other day. Bill could come back anytime and you and I both know he's armed."

"You don't really think he'd attack us, do you? Everyone in the neighborhood knows him. He would never get away with it!"

"Are you sure? Have you seen the police since that idiot in the park tried to arrest us? I haven't."

Madison frowned. "No. But that doesn't mean they don't exist. Or that they won't be coming through here."

"The police have other things to worry about besides a middle-class neighborhood in a good part of town. Think about it. Between what your mom said she heard and that guy who fought with the cop in the park, it sounds like there's riots all over downtown. If that's true, the police already have their hands full."

He pushed off the couch and picked up the bat, patting his palm with the barrel. "Think about it. Riots. Fires. Prisons running out of food and water. Jails at capacity with people awaiting trial. There's no way courts are working. Without janitors and cooks and suppliers, there are a whole lot of bad people out there ready to explode."

He swung the bat in a practice swing. "I wouldn't want to be a cop right now."

Peyton had a point. Once they were cocooned inside her parents' house, Madison had pushed all thoughts of the deteriorating outside world from her mind. But it was all still there.

Grocery stores. Gun and pawn shops. Restaurants with stocked kitchens and storerooms. So many vulnerable places. So many windows waiting to be smashed. All it took was one enterprising individual and then the rest would follow.

How long before the more dangerous parts of town turned into a free-for-all? Had it happened already? Were they next?

"How much of a target are we?"

Peyton scrunched up his face as he thought. The

motion reminded Madison of their days spent hovering over plants in the greenhouse. A wrinkled nose was a sure sign Peyton was lost in thought.

Madison smiled at the memory, but it was fleeting. She wondered about all the college kids who were partying for spring break in Southern California and Mexico. How many were still alive? How many would ever make it home?

At last, Peyton answered. "I don't know. But Bill saw the supplies in the Jeep and he thinks we have more. He said as much at the meeting. Who knows who overheard and is thinking of ways to break in."

He glanced up at the oversized picture window. "Do you all have any spare plywood lying around?"

Madison scanned her memory. "Not that I can think of."

"We need to secure the window. It's too exposed."

She glanced around. "We could push the entertainment center in front of it. The back is solid wood."

Peyton turned toward the large television cabinet and nodded. "That should work. Want to help?"

"Sure." Madison walked over and took up position on one side of the cabinet. "I hope you're prepared to take the laboring oar on this. I remember my dad complaining about it almost throwing out his back."

Peyton lowered into a squat, his hands braced on either side of the unit. "Where do you think he is right now?"

Madison couldn't think about her dad. She changed the subject. "Let's get this moved, okay?"

"On three. On, two, three."

Ugh. Madison lifted, using all of her leg and back strength, but she could barely get her side off the ground. Payton on the other hand, picked his side up with ease and began to drag it toward the window.

Madison limped along after him, half-scooting, half-carrying the monster shelving unit the few steps to the window. She set her side down in a massive thud, practically dropping it the last few inches. She stood up and groaned. "Remind me to never do that again."

"I didn't think it was too bad." Peyton stood back and eyed it, confirming the wood covered the glass. "It looks a little off center. Do you want—"

"No!" Madison almost shouted her refusal before flopping down onto the couch. "I'm not touching that thing. You want to move it, be my guest."

Peyton shrugged and went to work, sliding the entertainment center a bit to the left, then to the right until he deemed it perfect. "That should do it."

"What was that noise? Is everything all right?"

Wanda walked into the living room, hair dripping wet and Fireball curled up in her arms. The friendly little cat mewled as he saw Madison and reached out a paw in hello.

She walked up and scratched him behind the ears until he squirmed in Wanda's arms. "We moved the entertainment center to block the front window."

Wanda's brow knit together. "Why? That was such a nice view."

"From outside, too. Anyone could have looked in to

see what we are up to. It's also easy to break. One well-aimed rock and we'd be breached."

"You don't think someone would do that, do you?" Wanda glanced around as if she could see through the walls. "The neighborhood seems so quiet and friendly. Apart from that one man, I suppose."

"Bill pointed a gun at us, Wanda. If he's willing to do that only a few days after the power is out, what do you think will happen in a few weeks?"

Wanda grew sheepish. "I don't know, do you? Have either of you thought about what we're doing and why?"

Madison stilled, confidence giving way to doubt. "Not really. When the power went out, we were all focused on getting here. Everything we did, every choice we made, was all about getting home. Now that we're here…"

"There isn't a manual for this sort of thing. No textbook to learn from. We're on our own." Peyton grabbed the bat from where he left it and took another practice swing.

Madison clutched at her middle as a chill rushed through her. "I'm worried about my mom and the others. Something's gone wrong, I can feel it."

"Do you really want to go searching for them? We can take Brianna's Jeep."

"But then everyone will know we're gone. The house will be exposed." Madison chewed on her lip. Each choice put them at risk: go and leave the house vulnerable, stay and hope her mom and friends made it home alive.

Was this what it would always be like from now on? Teetering on the edge of a decision, not knowing whether to step back or jump?

Life a week ago was stable, dependable, safe. Now Madison didn't know whether the neighbor was about to shoot the lock off her front door or if her mother was trapped in a Walmart across town or somewhere on the road needing her help.

And her father...

Pushing her father out of her mind had become an art form. Where was he? Hong Kong? Seattle? The Sacramento Airport? Was he even alive?

Madison snorted back a wave of emotion and the tears that threatened to flow along with it. She didn't have time to break down. She didn't have time to be weak and afraid. Peyton and Wanda and fuzzy little Fireball needed her.

Her mom and Brianna and Tucker needed her.

The world might be going to hell in a handbasket, but Madison wasn't going to hop in and ride it down. She exhaled and straightened her back. "Let's root through the garage and see if we can't find something to secure the back windows. We need to make it as difficult as possible to break in."

"What about your mom?" Peyton's face creased with sympathy. Madison's mom had been a surrogate mother to Peyton for the last couple years. She knew he worried, too.

"She's a strong woman. I have to trust that she'll find a way to make it home."

Wanda stepped back to let Madison and Peyton

pass. As she did so, Fireball squirmed out of her arms. He landed on his paws with a soft thud and scampered into the kitchen.

Madison smiled. "You want to help us secure the house? How about you chase all the mice away?"

"Maybe we should train him to catch them, instead. We might need the protein."

"Don't be gross."

"I bet they taste just like chicken."

As Madison launched a soft punch at Peyton's shoulder, Fireball lowered into a crouch. His mouth opened and he hissed at the sliding glass door.

"What's he doing?"

"I don't know. Maybe he sees his reflection."

Madison turned to Wanda. "Turn off the lantern."

The woman rushed over to the kitchen table and flicked the lantern off. As darkness descended on the Sloane house, Fireball hissed again.

Madison peered out into the night. *Oh, no*. "Peyton, get the shotgun. There's someone in the yard."

CHAPTER NINE

MADISON

Sloane Residence
9:00 p.m.

"Are you sure?"

Madison nodded, clutching at Peyton's arm as they ducked around the corner. "The fence doesn't move on its own."

"How many were there? Did they have weapons? Were they just looking around or trying to break in?" Peyton shot questions rapid-fire into the dark, but Madison shook her head.

"I don't know. I only saw one, but that doesn't mean anything. We need to get ready. No matter how many are out there, we have to keep them out."

Wanda exclaimed under her breath. "I'm not cut out for this. First at George's place, now here. Please tell me you aren't going to shoot anyone today."

Madison blinked. "Who shot someone?"

Wanda muttered. "No one. Just forget I said anything. What can I do to help?"

"Can you get your revolver?" Peyton inched forward, head poking around the corner to scope out the backyard.

"It's in the guest room. I'll have to walk right by the door. What if someone sees me?"

"It's a risk we'll have to take." Madison exhaled. "Get it and meet us back here."

"All right." Wanda took off, rushing past the sliding door and heading toward the hallway.

"I'll get the shotgun. It's in the living room." Peyton began to move, but Madison reached out, clutching at his arm. "Be careful."

"I will." He handed her the bat and took off.

Madison wrapped her fingers around the shaft, nails digging into the grip as she steadied her nerves. *Please just be a nosy neighbor or a man out looking for his dog.* Not a thief. Burglar. Predator.

After the first few hisses, Fireball ran off, presumably hiding beneath a bed or otherwise making himself scarce. If only Madison could transform him into a lion, a massive wild counterpart to his little flame-colored self.

But Fireball wouldn't be coming to her rescue. No, Madison, Peyton, and Wanda were on their own. Two college kids and a fifty-something librarian. Not the best trained defense force around, but beggars couldn't be choosers.

Madison steeled herself. They needed to be ready to do whatever necessary. She clutched the bat tighter and eased toward the sliding glass door. She couldn't stop a rock, but she could stop a person. She readied the bat and waited.

"Any movement out there?"

Peyton's voice made her jump. As her heart slowed down from heart attack levels, she shook her head. "I can't see anything. It's too dark."

"Should I go out there and scare them off?"

"No. You could get shot."

"So we just wait for whoever is out there to break in?"

"What choice do we have? I'm not putting you at risk. There could be ten people, all armed with guns out there for all we know."

Peyton didn't respond right away. After a moment, he mumbled a curse. "Wanda must be hiding under the bed."

"Maybe she's keeping Fireball company."

Peyton snorted. "If she's not going to be out here, then she should give us her gun. It's no use to anyone tucked away in the guest room."

"I can't ask her to do that, and you know it. Maybe when my mom gets back..." If she gets back. *No.* Madison couldn't think that way; she wouldn't.

Her mom and Brianna and Tucker would be coming back. They were just held up. Joe must have needed help or Walmart had more supplies than they could fit in the car or they came across someone her mom knew.

There were a million innocent reasons for them to be late; she wouldn't think about the bad ones. She handed Peyton the bat. "Trade you."

He handed her the shotgun. "Brianna loaded it yesterday. All the ammunition we have is already in the gun. When you run out, that's all there is."

Madison nodded. Five shells. She would have to make them count. She inhaled and exhaled, counting with every cycle. *One. Two. Three. Four.* Whoever was out there didn't seem in a hurry. *Five. Six. Seven.*

"Maybe you're right. We could both go outside. One in the front, one in the back, case the place."

"It's too risky."

Madison and Peyton went back and forth, debating what to do, until a scream shocked them both still. Madison reached for Peyton. "Was that…?"

"Wanda."

"Let's go." Madison leapt up from her crouch, ignoring the risk, and ran toward the guest room.

"Wanda! Wanda!" Her voice carried down the hall, bouncing off the closed door and echoing back to her.

Another scream. This time more fear than surprise, the tone higher, the terror too real, too close.

Madison sucked in a breath, her own heart beating like a butterfly against glass, bruising and insistent. She reached the bedroom door two steps ahead of Peyton fueled by adrenaline and panic. Lunging for the door handle, she twisted and pulled.

Locked.

Damn it. What was she hiding from? Them? No one who wanted to break in would stop at a locked bedroom door. Madison hammered on the wood, ignoring the pain radiating up her arm as she slammed the side of her hand against the grain.

"WANDA!"

Peyton added his own deep voice to her shouts. "Wanda! Unlock the door! It's us! Wanda!"

He hammered a foot above Madison's fist, his beats as frantic as Madison's own.

"Why would she lock us out?" Madison tried the door handle again, yanking and twisting as she added her foot to bang on the door.

Another scream from inside and Madison turned to Peyton. "Can you knock it down?"

He blinked in slow motion, staring at the door as he thought it over. "I can try."

Madison backed up until she brushed the hallway as Peyton readied himself. Charging at the locked door like a linebacker, shoulder down, arm braced, he rushed past her. He slammed into the door and wood splintered, but it held. Peyton staggered back.

"Are you all right?"

He rubbed at his shoulder. "Yeah. Let me try again."

"Maybe we——"

Before she could finish, Peyton launched himself again, running faster and jumping into the door with all his strength. The upper hinges split from the frame, canting the door at an awkward angle, but the stubborn thing still stayed locked.

Peyton stood up, cradling his arm. "I think I dislocated my shoulder."

Madison couldn't believe this was happening. What

was going on inside that bedroom? Why hadn't Wanda let them in?

She cupped her hands around her mouth and shouted through the gap in the door and the frame. "Wanda! It's Madison. You've got to let us in. Please!"

As her voice edged into begging, Madison leaned against the door, resting her head on the wood. She turned her head to the side and stilled. *Is that…?*

With a start, she pulled back. "I hear crying."

"What?" Peyton stepped closer, still clutching at his arm and shoulder. "Is it Wanda?"

"I think so." Madison leaned back in, straining to listen. "Wanda? Are you all right? Whatever has happened, it's okay. We can get through it together. All you have to do is open the door."

Madison didn't know what more she could do. At some point, Wanda would either have to open the door, or they would have to go outside and try to break in through the single window. As she opened her mouth to voice her plan, the door knob rattled.

"Wanda?" She stepped back as the door creaked open. "Are you—"

One look at Wanda and Madison's tongue turned to a cinder block inside her mouth. Her shirt hung loose and torn, exposing a giant swath of skin across her middle. A bruise already purpled around her left eye, swelling the skin and forcing the eyelid shut.

One free hand trembled in the air as Wanda pointed inside the bedroom. "I…I didn't…I tried…he…"

She trailed off, the stops and starts of an explanation dying before anything coherent came out. Peyton eased past Madison. He wasn't waiting for any explanation. As he came around Wanda's side he stopped and whipped his head in Madison's direction.

His eyes confirmed Madison's fear. "What did you do? Is he dead?"

Oh, no. Madison slipped around Wanda and came to stand next to Peyton. A man half-sat, half-reclined on the floor, eyes closed, arms limp and floppy. Blood oozed from a gash on the top of his head, turning his blond hair into a matted, sticky mess. She swallowed.

"Wanda, what happened?"

Wanda's mouth opened and closed like a fish out of water.

"Did he attack you?"

She nodded.

"Did you hit him?"

Her head bobbed. "W-With the gun. I didn't m-m-mean to kill him."

Madison exhaled and clasped her hands together to steady them as she knelt at the man's side. He looked about her mother's age, mid-forties, maybe a few years younger. Pale skin, no wrinkles in his relaxed state. With his khaki pants and polo he didn't look like a criminal. He looked... like a neighbor.

She reached for his neck, pressing her fingers against the squishy side. *Thank God.* "He's not dead. Just unconscious."

Peyton mumbled a thanks beneath his breath. "What do we do with him?"

Madison stared down at the man. As much as she

hated to admit it, they couldn't let him go. Not after Wanda almost killed him.

If the police still existed in some fashion, or the other neighbors found out… It could mean the end of their safety. The end of the little fiefdom they had worked so hard to cobble together. Without her mom there to defend them, Madison couldn't begin to imagine how badly it could go.

At last, Madison lifted her head and met Peyton's troubled stare. "Find some tape and bind his arms and legs. We need to keep this contained."

CHAPTER TEN

WALTER

Cabin in Northern California
8:00 p.m.

Walter turned around, a dust-covered tin in each hand. "Tell me you like sardines."

Drew sat up just enough on the couch to scope out the stash. "Aw man, seriously? A whole cabinet full of sardines? Gross."

"Don't knock 'em 'til you try them." Walter tossed a tin at Drew and the man managed to catch it, only half-falling off the couch in the process.

"You're serious?"

"Indeed, I am. There have to be fifty tins up here, all a few years old. We can eat a couple and if the owner of the cabin shows up, he or she won't even miss them."

"You seriously still care about the owner of this

place? Look around. Every surface is covered in an inch of dust. Whoever owns it hasn't been here in years. We don't need to worry about eating an expired stash of sardines."

Walter exhaled. "Humor me, okay?"

"Fine." Drew stood up and made a show of hobbling over.

As he sat down at the table, Walter motioned to his feet. "How are the blisters?"

"Terrible. I don't know how I'm going to hike out of here tomorrow."

"Duct tape." Walter popped the top on the can and the pungent odor of the fish hit his nostrils. He scooped an oil-coated fillet out with his finger and popped it in his mouth. "There's got to be some around this place."

Drew watched him eat like he'd just chomped down on someone's eyeball, the horror of it contorting his mouth with every chew. "How is tape going to help? I don't have a hole in my shoes or socks."

Walter swallowed down the tasty morsel before scooping out another. "Simple. We duct tape your feet. The blisters will stop hurting then."

"But what happens to them? If my feet are all covered in tape, how will they get better?"

"They won't. But you want to get home, right? Sometimes life is crap. You have to suck it up." Walter slurped down the rest of the tin, dripping every last bit of oil into his mouth, before leaning back. "I love a good sardine."

Drew shook his head. "I knew you were crazy, but I had no idea how deep the psychosis went."

Walter laughed—a true, belly-shaking, wrinkle-generating, laugh. Something he hadn't done since the power went out. "So tell me about you, Drew. We've been co-pilots off and on for years, but I don't know much more than you wear prissy shoes and don't like the best fish to come out of a can."

Drew laughed and shook his head. "Not much to tell. I wanted to be a pilot since forever, so as soon as I graduated, I started saving up. Worked everything from bus boy to lawn mower and put myself through flight school."

"No debt?"

"Some that I'm still paying off. Or, was, anyway." Drew glanced down at his hands. "I met this amazing girl last year. Anne." Drew smiled, but Walter could see the fear in his eyes. "We were supposed to get married next month. At a golf course up in Granite Bay."

Walter nodded. The more he could open Drew up about his past and the woman he loved, the more Drew would see the importance of their current mission.

Getting home could be the only objective. Not rest or recovery. Not camping out in the forests of Northern California like a pair of overgrown Boy Scouts while the world fell down around them. Home mattered. Family mattered.

He motioned at Drew's unopened can. "You should eat."

Drew glanced down at it, hesitating. "I'm not a big seafood fan."

"You need the calories. Believe me, there's a whole hell of a lot worse stuff you could be eating."

"I take it you know from experience."

Memories of SERE school filled his mind, but Walter just smiled. "Yep. So open that damn can and eat some fish."

Drew frowned, but did as Walter asked, peeling back the lid of the tin before digging out a fillet. "You really just pop the whole thing in your mouth?

Walter nodded.

Drew scowled as he opened his mouth, the tendons in his neck popping out as he braved a bite. You'd think the man was about to swallow a live scorpion.

As Drew chewed, Walter brought the conversation back around. "So how did you and Anne meet?"

"You wouldn't believe it if I told you."

"Try me."

Drew managed to swallow down another fish before leaning back in his chair. "She ran into me."

Walter raised an eyebrow. "What's so special about that? It happens everyday."

"While carrying a three-layer chocolate cake. She was the catering assistant for my best friend's wedding." Drew grinned. "His bride still won't forgive me for smashing a thousand-dollar wedding cake."

"But it was an accident."

"Try explaining that to a woman wearing forty pounds of hand-beaded silk while you're wiping frosting off your eyelashes and picking bits of cake out of a hot chick's hair."

"Anne?"

"The one and only." Drew sat up. "Even covered in

white frosting and chocolate cream filling she was the most beautiful thing I'd ever seen. I asked her out right then, and the rest is history."

As soon as the words slipped out, Drew frowned. He leaned forward, elbows on the table, as he worked his jaw back and forth. At last, he glanced up. "Do you think she's all right?"

Walter wanted more than anything to tell the man sitting across from him, yes, your fiancée is fine. But he couldn't lie. "There's not a minute that goes by that I'm not thinking about my wife and daughter and whether they are okay. Madison is in college at UC Davis and Tracy works close to downtown at a small library."

He swallowed hard. "For all I know my daughter never made it out of school and is stuck on campus with no power, no running water, nothing but her wits and a ten by ten doom room to survive in."

"And your wife?"

"I have to believe she's still alive. I think she knew about the potential for this sort of thing. The only text she sent me that went through told me to come home. That things could be worse than I thought."

Walter balled his hand into a fist. He was so full of regret over his choices the day the grid failed. He should have gone with his gut and feigned an illness, refused to fly, walked out of the airport, and gone straight home.

Instead he sat in the captain's chair and flew a plane into the great unknown and watched as the lights blinked out for as far as he could see. "If I don't have faith and hope, then what do I have?"

Drew nodded slowly. "Anne works all over the city. She drives a delivery van from Rocklin to Elk Grove. If the power went out when she was on a job…" His voice cracked and Drew paused to run a hand through his hair. "She could be anywhere. She could be hurt, hungry, afraid, and I'm not there to protect her. I'm not there to——"

Walter reached out and put a hand on Drew's arm. "All we can do is work to get home as quickly as possible. If Anne isn't home when you get there, you can start a search. Go to her work, break in if you have to. Find her schedule, track her down. Cars still work. You can do what we talked about earlier and siphon gas if you have to."

With every word of encouragement Walter uttered a little life came back into Drew's eyes. "You're right. I can't give up."

"That's the spirit." Walter didn't tell Drew all the other thoughts inside his head. The bad ones. The horror of the future without electricity that he saw every time he closed his eyes.

Over the past twenty years family farms vanished like smoke up and down the Central Valley. Giant, corporate behemoths bought the land and converted self-sustaining operations into one-crop mega-farms built on the back of irrigation and fertilizer and chemicals.

He didn't begrudge them. Profitable businesses meant jobs and food and security when times were good. But without power, those farms couldn't survive. Without factories making the fertilizer and power running the massive irrigation systems, the crops would wither in a matter of days.

Every time Madison came home from college on break she talked about the advances in farming and how it had become as tech-savvy an enterprise as mobile phones and computers and cars.

People didn't get their fresh vegetables and meat from their backyard or even the farmer's market anymore. They got it from a shelf in the nearest grocery store. When those shelves didn't refill themselves, what would all the people do?

Rural communities might band together, he supposed. But a place as large as Sacramento with half a million people in the city itself and another two million clustered around the outside?

No one stood a chance. He pushed back his chair and sighed. "We need to get home. The faster we get there, the sooner we can pack up and leave."

Drew looked like he'd just swallowed a lemon. "Leave? Why?"

"Safety. Lack of resources. A million other reasons. It won't be safe there. We'll have to move out, find somewhere secluded, and start over."

Drew shook his head. "Sometimes I don't know who the hell you are."

Walter shrugged. "I'm the same man I've always been. Only now, the stakes have changed."

Drew opened his mouth to say something when a noise startled them both. Walter rushed to the lantern and turned it off.

"Did you hear that?"

Walter hushed Drew and ran to his bag. "Grab your things. If that's what I think it is, we'll need to make a run for it."

CHAPTER ELEVEN

WALTER

CABIN IN NORTHERN CALIFORNIA
9:00 p.m.

"WHAT'S GOING ON? IS SOMEONE OUT THERE?"

For once, Walter wished Drew would just take his advice. "Shut up. Do you want them to hear us?" He slung his bag over his shoulder and crept toward the front door. "We'll try and go out the front first. If they're far enough away, they won't see us."

"And if they do?" Drew's voice came out muffled as he worked on securing his things.

"Run like hell."

"I was afraid you'd say that."

Walter moved toward the front door, hoping Drew could see him in the dark. He held up his fist to halt. "If they start shooting, just run. Try to head south, but if you get confused, it's okay. What's important is that you don't get shot."

The ragged exhale of the air in Drew's lungs was the only reply. *Better than nothing.* Walter paused beneath the front window, rising up until his eyes cleared the sill. Somewhere out there at least two, if not more, men were approaching. It didn't take years of training and experience to hear the sounds of laughter and raucous carrying on, but Walter was thankful for his background all the same.

If only he had the appropriate gear.

From his vantage point, he could barely make out the hood of a car—late model, four-door sedan of some sort—with the trunk up. A light beam bounced around behind it, intermittently darting in the cabin's direction and then back to the trunk. If he slowed his breathing, he could hear voices, but couldn't make out the words.

As Walter tried to count the number of intruders, the trunk slammed and the flashlight beam lit up the car. *Oh, shit.*

"We need to go out the back. We can crawl through the window."

"What's wrong? How many are there?"

"Too many. Let's go."

Walter counted five men. All solid, with beer guts and thick necks and at least two shotguns slung over shoulders. One retired lieutenant colonel and a civilian pilot were no match for a car full of hunters in the forest.

He eased the lock shut on the front door and motioned for Drew to head toward the back. They needed to get the hell out of there before those guys got inside.

"What happened to tough guy Walt who punches first?"

"This isn't one I can win. Get moving. We don't have much time."

As they neared the window, the voices out front picked up.

"I mean it, Travis. This is the end of the whole goddamn world. It's gonna be just like them TV shows I keep tellin' you 'bout. Just wait."

Drew shoved his bag through the window and lifted one foot.

Walter stared at the man's sock in disbelief. "Where are your shoes?"

"In my bag. I can't put them on. We didn't find the duct tape, remember?"

Lord have mercy, this man is going to get me killed. Walter practically shoved Drew through the window after that, following up with his bag before Drew even cleared out of the way.

As he lifted himself up to ease through the frame, the front door handle jiggled. He slipped through just as the door swung open.

"Welcome to it, boys. It's the Shangri-La of Six Rivers forest."

"It's a dump."

"Watch it now, or you're gonna find yourself strung up outside by your toes. I paint your face in honey and I bet all the bears'll come after you."

"Shut up, Billy. I ain't lettin' nobody do nothin' like that."

"You ain't the one with the shotgun now, are ya?"

Walter pushed Drew toward the rail as the men inside carried on. They needed to get as far away from the cabin as possible before anyone noticed they had been there. After slinging his bag back over his shoulder, he jumped the rail and landed with a thud on the ground. Drew followed, wincing as he landed in shoeless feet.

"Hey! Hold up. What's all this shit? I thought you told me this place was empty?"

Oh, no. Walter pointed. "Run, Drew. Get at least a hundred yards into the trees before you turn south."

"Which way is south?"

The voices from inside turned to shouts. "Someone's been in here!"

"Get me that damn lantern."

"Billy! Get the gun, boy!"

"Run!" Walter took off, dragging Drew a few steps until the man got it together enough to move on his own. Thank goodness Walter's change of clothes included a dark shirt, otherwise he would be as easy to spot as a white rabbit in the forest.

Every step got them farther away from the bad end of a pair of shotguns and the crazy fools now occupying the cabin. Walter couldn't take on five guys with weapons, even if he'd been twenty years younger and well-rested. The only thing to do was run and hope like hell those overweight guys back there couldn't keep up or aim well enough to make it not matter.

"Where are we going?" Drew huffed out the question between haggard breaths. "I can't see anything. I'm going to hit a tree."

"Just keep going. We've got to get far enough away that we aren't worth the chase. A mile at least."

"You're serious?" Drew groaned and slipped back half a step. "I can't go that far, man. My feet are torn to shreds."

"You'd rather be shot?"

"No."

"Then run faster." Walter grabbed Drew by the arm and forced him to keep up the grueling pace. Sweat slicked his back, dripped off his nose, and stung his eyes with every step, but Walter wasn't stopping.

His wife and daughter needed him home alive. Getting shot a three-hour drive from home wasn't how he was going to end it all.

Sounds of voices could still be heard behind them, but the shouts grew fainter the farther they ran. The thought they might escape made him push harder, run faster.

As they ducked around a large pine, Walter's foot caught on a hidden root and he stumbled. His hands shot out on instinct, bracing for a fall, but he managed to keep himself upright. Drew wasn't so lucky.

The man fell, landing hard on the ground as his bag flew over top of him and into a pile a leaves.

"Drew! Are you okay? Drew!" Walter crouched beside him, running his hands over his back, feeling for lacerations.

Drew groaned and rolled onto his side. "I think I

chipped a tooth." His former co-pilot sat up, feeling around his face for cuts. "Help me up, would you? We should keep going."

Walter stood and held out his arm. As Drew stood, he cried out and lifted his left foot. "Damn it. I did something, Walt. I don't know if it's broken or sprained, but my ankle is messed up."

"Can you walk?"

Drew tried to put some weight on his foot, but he shook his head. "I don't think so."

Walter bit down hard on the inside of his cheek. He couldn't carry Drew and they weren't far enough away from the cabin to be safe. They needed to keep moving.

What on earth were they going to do? Walter helped Drew ease back down onto the ground. "Rest your foot up on the log. You need to elevate it to keep the swelling down."

Drew did as he was told. "What are we going to do?"

Walter wiped the sweat and grime from his brow. "I don't have a clue. We need to keep moving to be safe. Maybe I can find a fallen limb you can use as a cane or a crutch. With enough time, I could make a litter and drag you."

"That sounds like fun."

"Any ideas Mr. Two Left Feet?"

"Hey! It was an accident!"

Walter held up his hands in apology as light caught his eye. It blinked out as quickly as it appeared.

"What was that?" Drew shifted, trying to spot it again. "There! Look! I think it's headlights!"

Drew was right. A car was working its way up the hill toward the cabin. It had to be a ways off, but it would pass them soon. Walter turned to Drew. "Stay here. I'm going to flag that vehicle down."

"What if it's the guys from the cabin?"

"It's a risk I have to take. You need medical attention and I can't get us out of here on my own. Stay put."

"What if you don't come back?"

"Then best of luck to you." Walter turned and took off for the road, running as fast as he could while keeping an eye out for fallen trees and branches. He couldn't repeat Drew's mistake.

He made it to the side of the road as the headlights came into full view. Without a moment's pause he threw up his hands, waving them in huge arcs. The vehicle slowed.

Walter didn't know if the car approaching was his death or salvation, but he didn't have a choice. He had to take the chance.

CHAPTER TWELVE

TRACY

WALMART

    3:00 p.m.

THERE HAS TO BE A WAY OUT OF HERE. TRACY EASED back behind the end cap and slipped the shotgun off her shoulder. She didn't want to use it. Shooting people wasn't going to be her MO.

No matter what happened, she would find a way to get out of there without firing a gun. Tracy wondered if Brianna and Tucker knew they weren't alone. Had either kid seen the newcomers? Or were they going about their business, filling carts and being teenagers?

She should give Tucker some credit; the boy was twenty, but it didn't matter. Nineteen, twenty, twenty-one —they were all less than half Tracy's age and still children. Madison might be brave with a good head on her shoulders and strong values, but that didn't give her life experience. It didn't give her the wisdom needed to make tough choices.

Tracy forced her breathing to stay even and unhurried. Terror wasn't something new to her. She had plenty of it growing up. The tightness in her chest. The feeling of exploding on the inside, but staying together on the outside; skin the only reason she didn't fly apart in a million jagged pieces.

Television shows always painted childhood as this idyllic time free from worry and fear. Tracy experienced the opposite. When her mother wasn't high, she was strung out. The days she disappeared, leaving nothing but a jar of peanut butter and dirty dishes, were good days.

The days she came back with strangers were the worst. Tracy pushed her memories away. Her experience growing up was one of the reasons she worked so hard to give Madison the best life. She needed to make sure it continued.

With her hands gripping the shotgun tight, Tracy eased forward, once again checking on the men in the aisle.

The aisle was empty.

Tracy's skin began to crawl. *They could be anywhere.* One aisle over. Across the store. Holding Tucker at gunpoint. Dragging Brianna out by her hair.

Tracy couldn't let anything happen to those two. With a deep breath she darted across the aisle, stopping behind the next end cap. She couldn't be more than twenty feet away from Brianna if she was still in guns and ammo.

Another deep breath and Tracy peeked around the corner. Empty. She ran for it without hesitating. Again, she looked, assessed, determined she could run for it, and went. One more round and Tracy could see the gun displays along the back wall.

Unfortunately, voices came along with them.

"What you think, Dave? How many can we fit in the truck?"

"Hell, all of 'em, dontcha think?"

The men laughed and Tracy cringed. They sounded close—too close. Where was Brianna? Had she heard them approach and hid? Had they already found her and knocked her out?

She had known about the risks coming here, but now Tracy wished they had all stayed home. If she had fought harder and argued with Madison more, maybe they wouldn't be here. Brianna and Tucker wouldn't be risking their lives and Tracy would know Madison was safe.

If they made it out of there alive, that was it. No more trips. No more runs. Whatever they had in the house would have to last.

If only it could last forever.

Tracy eased back into the aisle and crept away from the voices. She would find Tucker first and circle back. If those men did have Brianna, she would need Tucker's help.

The farther she backpedaled, the easier it became to breathe. Unable to hear the two men debating what guns to take and what to leave behind, Tracy could focus on the other noises in the warehouse: the intermittent squeak of her shoes on the concrete floor, the chirp of a bird trapped somewhere along the roofline, the clank of a can as it landed in a shopping cart.

Tucker.

Tracy headed toward the noise, bypassing bedding and clothing and a whole display of DVDs and CDs. The food portion of the warehouse spanned an entire side, with canned goods positioned up near the front. Thank goodness Tracy shopped there now and again, otherwise she would never find her way.

As she passed the aisles of freezer cases, the noxious smell of thousands of pounds of rotting food forced her to cover her nose and mouth. It wouldn't take long before such a smell attracted vermin, if it hadn't already. It made her think about all the waste.

The pounds and pounds of food companies made and packaged into plastic bags and cardboard boxes and shipped to stores like Walmart and Target and Costco in giant refrigerated trucks. All spoiled and worthless.

At least the canned goods would keep forever. Tracy slowed as she reached the first aisle of shelf-stable products. Tucker should be right around the corner, she hoped. Adjusting her grip on the shotgun, Tracy inched toward the aisle, peeking around the corner. She caught the last glimpse of a person before he disappeared behind the end cap.

Rats.

Tracy couldn't tell if she'd seen Tucker, one of the strangers, or even Brianna. She glanced behind her. Standing in the wide-open space a few aisles from checkout increased her vulnerability. Too exposed. Too easy to pick off.

She needed cover. She would just have to take a chance that the person she saw was friendly. With a deep breath, Tracy rushed down the aisle, half-running, half-sliding across the floor. As she reached the end, she slowed, turning the corner at almost a walk.

Not slow enough. As she turned, she collided with a body. A warm, solid body holding an armful of full-size cans. A few tumbled from his arms like potatoes from a sack.

"Mrs. Sloane! What are you doing?"

Tracy grabbed Tucker by the arms and shushed him. "Quiet! There's someone else inside the store."

"I know. Brianna's over in the hunting department living out her commando dream."

"No! I saw two men. I don't think they know we're here."

Another can fell from Tucker's arms and landed smack on the top of Tracy's foot. She stifled a yelp and grabbed her foot, hopping to relieve some of the ache.

"Sorry." Tucker set the rest of the cans down. "Where's Brianna?"

"I don't know. I tried to find her in the guns and ammo area, but the two men beat me to it. It didn't sound like they spotted her. Have you seen her at all?"

Tucker shook his head. "No."

"Then we need to come up with a plan to find her and get out of here before those guys spot us."

"If we do find Brianna, she won't leave without the weapons."

"She won't have a choice."

Tucker hesitated. "We could... hurt them."

Tracy frowned. "Shooting someone should be the last resort, not the first idea that pops into our heads."

Tucker turned and glanced down the aisle. "What if they have her already?"

"If those men lay one finger on Brianna, or you for that matter, I won't hesitate to pull the trigger. But I'm not going to shoot first."

"Promise me you won't let anything happen to Brianna. She's the closest thing to family I have. My parents are dead. I was an only child. If it weren't for Brianna and her family... I don't know where I'd be."

Tracy gave Tucker's arm a squeeze. "You probably wouldn't be hiding behind a display shelf of canned salmon plotting how to sneak out of a dark Walmart in the middle of the afternoon."

Tucker snorted back a laugh. "You're probably right."

Enough chitchat. Time to go. Tracy gave Tucker one more reassuring pat. "Okay. Let's head toward the hunting department. We can check every aisle between here and there. Stay low and close to the shelves, but don't knock anything off. We need to be as quiet as possible."

"What happens when we find her?"

"If she's alone and they haven't spotted us, we backtrack and sneak out the front. Those guys must have come in that way, otherwise they would have spotted the car."

"And if she's not alone?"

"Then we fight like hell until we get her back."

Even in the dim light, Tracy could read the expression on Tucker's face. He trusted her. He thought she would be the ticket to safety and her ideas were the ones to follow. If he only knew that she was as clueless as the rest of them.

Tracy hadn't lived through very many apocalypses, and as bad as her childhood was, it didn't count. Any idea she came up with should be vetted by people smarter and wiser. But no one was here offering up his or her services. She had to rise to the occasion. She had to be the leader.

Tucker and Brianna were counting on her. She couldn't mess this up.

"Let's go aisle by aisle. Each of us walking up and down. If she's hiding, maybe she'll see us and come out. If she's not, then we can eliminate that aisle from the search.

"Ready?" She waited as Tucker bent down to pick up a soup can in each hand.

"Let's do this."

CHAPTER THIRTEEN

TRACY

Walmart

5:00 p.m.

Why did Walmart have to be so big? After searching three quarters of the store with one eye out for the two men whooping it up in the guns department, Tracy's hope waned. Wherever Brianna hid herself away to escape the intruders, Tucker and Tracy couldn't find her.

"Maybe she curled up in the blankets and towels and took a nap."

"With two guys firing handguns into the same department?"

"You have a point." Tucker hunched down close to the end of the aisle as another shot popped off.

At least the two men cared more about goofing off than they did about scoping out the rest of the store.

93

Every few minutes one of them would shout about the latest gun he'd loaded and the other would dare him to shoot it.

From three aisles away, Tracy had watched them drink a case full of warm beer, crush the cans on their foreheads, and joke how they would turn the whole bedding department into one giant shooting range.

She thought they were only kidding until one wheeled a shopping cart full of pillows and comforters into the middle of the store and took a sharpie to them, creating wobbly circle targets on every zipped-up plastic bag. Instead of prepping for the future, they were wasting ammunition and the batteries of half the lanterns in the sporting goods department just to have some stupid fun.

Tracy inhaled and the acrid smell of fertilizer itched her nose. They were camped out in the garden department, as far away from those trigger-happy fools as they could get. But they still needed to find Brianna and get home.

Reaching up, Tracy pushed her damp hair away from her face before tugging out the loosened ponytail and fixing it. If they ever made it out of there alive, she would either jump in the first pool they came across or sacrifice a bottle of water just to wash her hair.

Tucker handed her a granola bar. "You should eat."

Tracy took the package from him, squinting to read the label. The garden section of the store received the most natural light from outside with clear windows and double doors to a small outside area. *Pure Organics Chocolate Banana Bar.* She glanced up.

"Where did you get this?"

Tucker made a face. "You do know we're in Walmart, right? There's a million of them back in aisle four."

"Right." All this time, Tracy had been focused on gathering supplies from her section, looking for Brianna, and trying to evade the two men. She forgot Tucker had been scouring food shelves. "Thanks."

She unwrapped the bar and ate, washing it down with a purple pastel Gatorade Tucker pulled out of a six-pack. How many sidelines did Tracy sit at over the years, cheering Madison on as she kicked a soccer ball down the field? How many snacks did she watch her daughter eat, unwrapping the little granola bar, breaking the seal on the sports drink so she could rehydrate?

Madison's elementary school alone housed a thousand kids. It, along with sixteen other schools, made up the district. Thousands of kids, all living in the city, wondering when the lights would come back on. How were their families surviving? How were they coping with this potential future?

Tracy finished the last bite and drained the bottle. *Food*. So simple, easy, and taken for granted. She turned to Tucker. "The only way we're going to find Brianna and get out of here is if we make a commotion. We're going to have to shout her out."

Tucker opened his mouth to respond when a gun shot cut him off. Apparently, the two men had moved onto shotguns. He tried again. "Those two idiots are drinking beer and shooting at bed-in-a-bag sets and stacks of pillows and we're going to let them know we're here? That's insane."

"Brianna won't leave without weapons, you said so yourself."

"I don't follow."

Tracy exhaled. While she chewed the granola bar, a plan had come to her. It might not work, but they didn't have a choice. Staying in the garden department of Walmart wasn't a permanent solution. "We need to set a trap. Lead those two into it and flush Brianna out all at the same time."

After a moment, Tucker nodded. "I get it. Okay."

"Do you have any ideas?"

Tracy could practically see the gears turning in Tucker's head. The science geek part of him was already drawing up plans. "I've got one, but it'll take some work. How do you feel about manual labor?"

"Whatever gets the job done."

He smiled. "Great. Then let's get started. We've got a lot of cans to move."

* * *

An hour later and they were ready. Tracy stepped back to marvel at their handiwork. "Do you think it will work?"

Tucker nodded. "Even if only fifty percent deploy, we should incapacitate them."

"Okay." Tracy wiped her sweaty palms on her jeans. "Let's do this." She picked up the shotgun from where she had left it on the now-empty shelf and smiled at

Tucker. "If something happens, grab Brianna and get out of here."

"All of us are making it out of here alive, Mrs. Sloane."

"It's Tracy, please."

"Fine." He rolled his eyes. "Tracy, you're going home today. Alive and without a single bullet hole. Is that better?"

Tracy laughed despite her rising fear. "Yes. Thanks, Tucker. Wish me luck."

"You don't need luck. You have guts."

Before any more doubt set in, Tracy took off, shotgun in one hand and a makeshift megaphone in the other. She thought of her favorite movie when she was a teenager and smiled before taking off, her feet pounding the concrete floor.

She shouted into the megaphone. "I wanna be an airborne ranger!"

As she turned another corner, she ran the barrel of the shotgun along a rack of cans, knocking them all to the floor. "I wanna live the life of danger!"

Visions of John Bender's hair blowing as he ran, his fingers trailing across the lockers of Shermer High, filled her mind. She smiled as she neared the main aisle, belting out the rest of the song, even when it veered away from the well-known cadence and into something as a teenage girl she blushed over.

At last, the two trigger-happy men began to shout. Tracy cleared the final aisle and there they were, countless beers into case number two, long guns in each hand. *Just stick to the plan, Tracy. Just stick to the plan.*

"Hey boys! Up for a little game? How about chase?" She took off, racing around the end cap as both men shouted again.

"Hey! Get back here!"

She didn't stop. "Come and get me!"

Their footsteps thundered behind her, four drunk and off-balance thuds for each of her two. *It's working.* Tracy kept just far enough ahead, knocking cans and boxes onto the floor as she neared the aisle set with the trap.

"Are you ready?" Tracy slowed as she entered the aisle, waiting until the men could see her before continuing. *Please Tucker, please be ready.* She raced past the spot of the trap, stopping three-quarters of the way down the aisle.

Huffing and out of breath, both men appeared. One had a lantern in his hand and he held it up while the other gripped his knees and sucked in labored breaths. "Hey pretty lady, why the chase?"

"To make the reward that much more special." She shook her backside and pushed up her chest. "You do want a reward, don't you?"

The one with the lanterns stepped forward, but the other man grabbed his arm. "It could be a trap."

The man with the lantern shrugged him off. "I don't care what it is. She's hot and I'm horny. You can wait here. I won't be long."

Tracy cursed under her breath. She needed both of them to come to her for this to work. After a moment's hesitation, she lifted her shirt. "Come on, honey, I've got more than enough for both of you. Unless you want your friend to have all the fun."

The holdout spat on the ground and Tracy forced the smile to stay on her face. She shimmed and dropped her shirt. "Clock's ticking."

At last, the man stepped forward. *Yes! Just keep coming.*

She counted off their steps like she was a ticking clock, but it was more for Tucker's benefit than anything. "One. Two. That's it, come and get me. I won't run anymore. I promise."

Both men advanced. "Three. Four. Only a little bit more. Come and give it to me." She pouted and blew them each a kiss, trying not to gag in the process.

"You sure about this, honey?"

"Of course I am."

Only a few more steps. *Come on, come on.* "Five, six, seven. That's it boys."

Two more feet and they were in position. *Please.*

The lantern-wielding man moved ahead of his friend. The other one reached out and grabbed his arm again. "Hey! She said we both get a chance. Who says you get to be first?"

"I'm not the one who hesitated. You're the one who didn't want to. You can have my sloppy seconds." He grabbed at his crotch and Tracy swallowed down the rising bile in her throat. *Just move!*

As they argued back and forth, they danced in and out of the target. Tracy was going out of her mind. Every second that ticked by, their goal slipped further and further away.

She did the only thing she could think of. "Hey! How about you quit arguing and you can both have a go. At the same time!"

Both men turned to her, slow-motion smiles spreading across their faces. "Hell, yes!"

As they took the last steps needed, Tracy shouted. "Now!"

Before she could blink, the wall of Rotel, all three thousand cans by Tucker's estimation, toppled. It started at the top, the first few raining down like oversized hail from above.

One of the men shouted and tried to move out of the way, but it was no use. The rest of the cans followed, a crescendo of noise and destruction. In seconds, the pair were buried beneath metal and hundreds of pounds of spicy tomatoes.

Tracy sucked in a lungful of air before bringing the megaphone back up to her mouth and yelling as loud as she could manage. "Brianna!"

CHAPTER FOURTEEN

MADISON

    7:00 p.m.

MADISON PACED BACK AND FORTH IN THE KITCHEN, A half-empty bottle of Gatorade in her hand. She wished it were beer or wine or even vodka. She didn't drink, but she could start. It was the apocalypse after all; age limits no longer applied.

Peyton appeared in the doorway with dark circles under his eyes. He rubbed his shoulder. "I'd give a very special body part to have an ice pack right now."

"Don't be gross."

"I'm not. I'm completely serious."

"How is he?" Part of Madison didn't want to know. Maybe if she didn't think about him, then the man duct taped and tied to the iron bed in the master bedroom would disappear.

"The same as twenty minutes ago. Passed out cold. His head wound seems to have stopped bleeding though, so that's good." Peyton hesitated. "I think. Is it good?" He shook his head and walked over to the stack of Gatorades. "I don't even know anymore."

Madison agreed. "Last week we were gearing up for midterms and talking about summer vacation."

"Now we're deciding what to do with a guy some librarian we don't even know tried to kill."

"If she'd been trying to kill him, she'd have used a bullet. She was scared and reacted. Are you telling me that if the situation were reversed you wouldn't have defended yourself?"

"I wouldn't have put myself in that position in the first place."

Madison sighed. It was easy for Peyton to say he wouldn't have reacted the same way, but when a strange man busts through the bedroom window and tries to punch your lights out, he's not there to introduce himself and invite everyone over for tea.

"Cut Wanda some slack. She's trying. If it weren't for her, you wouldn't be clean, remember?"

"Peyton grimaced as he surveyed his fingernails. "I'm not sure we'll ever be clean again."

Madison ran her hand through her hair. The strands still held onto enough grease to make her nose scrunch. "None of that matters. We need to figure out what to do with him. We can't keep him tied up in there forever. His friends will come looking for him."

"How do you know he has friends? He could be a loner. Does he look familiar?"

Madison exhaled. "I don't really know my parents' neighbors." Oh, how she wished her mom and dad were back home. Thanks to the break-in and resulting prisoner, Madison had temporarily put her mom's absence out of her mind. But thinking about the neighbors brought it back full force.

"They'll be all right, Madison. Your mom is tough as nails. If they've run into trouble, she'll find a way to bring Brianna and Tucker home."

"Thanks." She managed a small smile.

"Guys?" Wanda called out from the living room. "I hate to interrupt, but there are headlights in the driveway."

"My mom!"

"Or someone looking for their friend." Peyton reached for the shotgun. "We can't be too careful."

Madison nodded and pulled Wanda's handgun out from her waistband. Ever since she almost bashed a man's head in, Wanda said she didn't want to touch it.

"I'll take up position in the hall. You get behind the entertainment center. At the first sign of trouble, shoot."

Peyton nodded and slipped behind the entertainment center as the lights out front shut off. Madison hid behind the corner of the wall leading to the bedrooms. *Please be my mom. Please.*

The door handle rattled, followed shortly by a knock. "Hey you jerks! Open up, it's us!"

Madison exhaled in relief and rushed to the front door. She threw it open and wrapped Brianna up in a bear hug. "You're all right!"

"No thanks to two frat boys who thought target

practice in an empty Walmart was the best way to waste ammo." She stepped back, her blonde curls sticking every which way, and pointed at the entertainment center. "Redecorating?"

Madison swallowed. "We had a bit of an incident."

"What? Is everyone okay?" Madison's mom, Tracy, appeared in the doorway.

Madison ran to her, hugging her even tighter than she'd hugged her roommate. "You came home."

"Of course I came home. But are you all right? What happened?"

"There's plenty of time to talk about it. Can I help haul in gear? Is Tucker okay?"

"He's fine, just collecting the things from the car. Unfortunately we don't have much. A few more guns, some boxes of ammo, and a bit of food, but we had to leave most of it behind."

Tucker entered the house then, an oversized black gun bag slung over his shoulder and a cardboard box in his arms. "We're lucky to be alive. Your mom really came through. I had no idea she could dance like that."

Madison raised her eyebrows, but her mom waved her off. "I'll fill you in later."

"Yes, you will."

Peyton shut and locked the front door. "The important thing is that everyone is home safe." He slapped Tucker on the back. "Nice to have you back, man."

"Good to be back." Tucker bumped Peyton in the shoulder and the big guy almost curled up into a ball. "Whoa. What happened to you? Is your arm broken?"

"I don't think so. Bruised really bad, though."

Madison exhaled. "After you all get something to eat and drink, we need to talk. We have a problem."

* * *

"WHAT DO YOU MEAN THERE'S A MAN TRAPPED IN MY bedroom?" Madison's mom's gaze darted from her daughter to Peyton to Wanda and back again.

No one volunteered.

"Is he alive? Dead? What happened?"

Peyton scratched at his ear. "He's alive, but he's got a nasty gash in the top of his head. Lost a bit of blood."

"Did he break in? Threaten you?"

Madison glanced at Wanda. The woman sat hunched over her bottle of room-temperature juice, a cardigan wrapped around her despite the heat. Her eye had swollen completely shut and the skin around it looked almost black. "Wanda should explain it."

Her mom turned to Wanda, waiting. After what seemed like forever, Wanda reached for her juice, turning the bottle around and around on the table. "We were all standing around, chitchatting in the kitchen when Madison saw someone in the backyard."

"Okay." Her mom sat forward in her seat, elbows on the table. "Then what?"

Madison glanced at Brianna and Tucker. They sat super close, hands wrapped around each other, listening and waiting. She was so thankful no one was seriously hurt. After Tucker and Brianna explained the drama that went down at Walmart, Madison knew how lucky they had been.

Wanda chewed on her lip. "Madison and Peyton rushed to turn out the lights and get the weapons. I... I ran to the bedroom. I was going to get my father's gun..."

"But?"

She swallowed a small sip of juice. "I panicked, locked the door, and stood there in the dark shaking like a leaf. When I saw him in the window outside, I froze. I thought if I didn't move, maybe he would just go away."

"He didn't." Peyton, obviously disgusted by the whole scene, stood up and walked over to the far window.

Wanda agreed. "He threw a rock through the window. Climbed in a minute later. I started screaming."

"When she screamed, we rushed that way, banged on the door, tried to get it open."

"That's when he hit me."

"And that's how I hurt my shoulder." Peyton glanced at Madison's mom. "You have some solid doors in this place, Mrs. Sloane."

She smiled, but it wasn't happy. "Sorry you got hurt."

Wanda spoke up. "I am, too. I never meant for this to happen. When the man crawled in through the window I pointed the gun at him, but he didn't stop. He... he laughed." She tucked the cardigan tighter around her shoulders. "After he hit me, I just reacted. I didn't think it would hurt him that bad. I just... I wanted him to leave me alone. To leave all of us alone."

Madison's mom reached across the table and patted Wanda's hand. The older woman wrapped her other fingers on top and squeezed. Something passed between them; Madison didn't know if it was an apology and acceptance or just an acknowledgment of what happened, but when her mom pulled back, her face softened.

"What matters is that we're all alive and mostly unharmed."

"But what do we do about him?"

Her mom shook her head. "I'm not sure yet. We'll need to wake him up. Find out what he knows and if he has any friends. Then we can decide."

Madison's eyes went wide. "You mean like an interrogation?"

Her mom shrugged. "I'd prefer to call it a question and answer period, but interrogation works."

Wow. Her friends had commented over and over about how tough her mom had been, but Madison hadn't appreciated it until now. She'd been the one to comfort Madison when she fell and scraped her knee. The mom who baked the best muffins on Saturday mornings and invited all of Madison's friends over for every long weekend and holiday.

Tracy Sloane was the most caring, welcoming woman Madison knew. And now she proved herself to have a backbone of steel. Madison sat a little taller on the kitchen chair. If she could grow up to be half as brave and strong as her mom, she would consider it a success.

Her mom pushed back from the table and stood.

"The guy is passed out cold. Let's get the window secure. There's some plywood in the garage. Then we can take shifts keeping watch, but otherwise, we should all try and get a good night's sleep. We can wake him up and figure out what to do in the morning."

Everyone around the table nodded.

"I'll take the first shift."

"Madison, are you sure, honey?"

Madison nodded.

"I'll take second shift." Brianna smiled at Madison. "I won't be able to sleep much anyway."

"All right. Thanks, girls. At the first sign of trouble, come get me."

"Don't worry, Mrs. Sloane, we'll be fine."

Madison's mom sighed. "We've been through this. I'll never get you kids to call me Tracy, will I?"

They all laughed and split up, some going to their sleeping bags, others to a last-minute drink from the counter. Madison headed toward her parents' bedroom. As she pushed open the bedroom door, the man they held prisoner came into view.

He groaned and shifted in his restraints.

Madison gripped the shotgun tighter and shut the door behind her. Could she shoot him if she had to?

Madison didn't know and she hoped she wouldn't have to find out.

CHAPTER FIFTEEN

WALTER

Forest of Northern California
10:00 p.m.

Walter waved his arms back and forth as he stood in the beam of the headlights. The brightness eclipsed his entire vision and for a moment he wondered if death came on like this: a blinding light followed by whatever came next.

Heaven. Hell. The end of the world.

He lowered his arms as the vehicle slowed. It pulled up alongside him and Walter exhaled in relief. Military. The emblem on the side read Army National Guard and beneath it in small block print, Eureka, CA. Walter stepped off the road and waited.

The passenger-side door to the Humvee opened and a kid who looked like he was playing dress up in his dad's closet stepped out. The insignia for a private covered his shoulder and Walter marveled. Either they let them in younger and younger or he really was getting old.

"Do you need assistance?" The kid didn't smile as he spoke, but he could tell from the way he stood, awkwardly gripping his gun in his left hand, that he didn't want to engage a hostile.

Walter nodded. "Yes, please. My friend tripped over a log about a hundred and fifty feet into the forest. He can't walk."

The private glanced around. "Do you have a car?"

"No. We're on foot. Trying to get to Sacramento."

Another man jumped out of the Humvee and approached.

"Sir, this man has a friend who's hurt in the woods and can't walk. He's requesting assistance to get him out."

The other guardsman nodded and stuck out his hand. "Staff Sergeant Hickman at your service."

Walter shook the man's hand. "Walter Sloane, USMC retired." He glanced back at the forest. The men from the cabin could still be chasing them. He needed the guardsmen to help and fast. "If you don't mind, I'm worried about my friend. We were chased by a bunch of thugs into the woods. They could still be looking for us."

The private glanced at his superior, waiting.

Hickman shouted at the vehicle. "Gortz, Mather, get out here and help us look for an injured civilian."

The two men responded in the affirmative as they clambered out. Walter pointed the way and with him guiding them through the brush, they located Drew in minutes. He still sat where Walter left him with his foot propped up on the log and a sorry look on his face.

The staff sergeant coordinated moving out. When they reached the side of the road, he turned to them both. "Let's get you two into the Humvee and checked out by the medic back at base camp."

Walter agreed. He'd never been so thankful to see a bunch of soldiers in his life.

DAY FIVE

CHAPTER SIXTEEN

WALTER

National Guard Armory, Eureka, CA
6:00 a.m.

Walter rubbed the sleep from his eyes as the private he'd met the night before handed him a steaming paper cup of coffee. He sipped it with thanks and tried to wake up.

It had taken at least an hour to reach the National Guard facility after Walter flagged the Humvee down. Then they had been shuffled inside and asked a few questions about where they were from and where they were headed.

When they were satisfied, a guardsman treated Drew's ankle injury and his bleeding blisters and sent him to a cot somewhere with a sleeping pill and a bottle of water. Walter had intended to stay awake long enough to learn what was happening out in the world, but he'd succumbed to the suggestion of a cot for himself and fell asleep as soon as his eyes closed.

Now he stood in the chilly coastal air, sipping bad coffee, just as clueless as he was the night before. He glanced at the private's name tape. "Private Lewis, is it?"

The kid nodded.

"Been with the Guard long?"

He shook his head. "Just finished training, sir. This is my first deployment."

What an introduction. Walter felt for the kid. He looked about the same age as his daughter. So young and inexperienced. He wondered where his daughter was and whether she possessed the same bewildered expression as Private Lewis.

"Thank you for stopping and picking us up. I don't know what we would have done if you hadn't come along."

The kid nodded his acceptance. "We were supposed to go to Portland to help out with the riots there, but we got called back just south of the border. Lucky for you we got forced off I-5 and onto the backroads."

It sounded familiar. "Where are you headed now?"

The kid hesitated. "My sergeant says Sacramento."

Walter almost spit out his sip of coffee. "Why? Did something happen?"

"It's real bad there. Riots. Looting. Even the prison caught fire."

Another guardsman walked up and joined the conversation midstream. "I heard all of downtown is burning and the south side is even worse. It's like Armageddon down there, man."

Walter reeled. If Sacramento was as far gone as they said, was his family even alive? He glanced at the other man's name tape. "Havers, is it?"

"That's my name."

"Do you know any more? What about the more established parts of town?"

"You mean the nicer ones?"

Walter nodded.

"As far as I know, they're on their own. Our job is to get that shit contained and keep it from spreading. What the rich people do inside their fancy houses and behind their gates isn't our problem."

Tracy wasn't waiting in a fancy house or behind a big gate for Walter to come home, but they didn't live in a bad part of town, either. He frowned. How would the National Guard contain anything? The power loss wasn't temporary. Nothing would get any better.

"How are you going to keep the violence from spreading? Are you hauling in aid? Food and water and temporary shelter?"

Havers laughed. "No, man. Not even close. We're supposed to set up a perimeter. No one in. No one out."

Walter blinked. "That's the plan?"

The kid nodded. "We're fencing off all the zones of unrest."

"You're locking them in?"

The other guardsman answered. "Let them all shoot each other. That's what Sergeant says. In a week, everyone will be dead one way or another. No point in getting shot for a hopeless cause."

Walter couldn't believe his ears. "What about all the

people still trapped in the city? There have to be thousands of good people stuck in the middle of the riots. Aren't you going to go rescue them?"

Havers snorted. "Who do you think we are? The Marines? Naw, man. You wanna risk your life, go ahead. We won't stop you."

He reached into his pocket and pulled out a photo. "I've got a little girl. She's four. I'm not going in there so some thug can put a bullet in my head."

Havers stuck the photo back in his pocket and continued. "This isn't just a California thing or a West Coast thing. It's national. Hell, it could be all over the world for all we know. The president is supposedly in some bunker somewhere barking out orders, but there's no one left to listen. The state government's a joke, the police are all gone. It's over. Everything is over."

Private Lewis kicked at the ground. "I heard since there's no more computers, we can't get paid. Everything used to go all automatic-like right into our bank accounts. No one knows how to do it the old-fashioned way."

Walter exhaled. It was as bad as he feared. Worse. "If you all aren't getting paid, why are you here?"

Havers spat on the ground. "That sergeant of ours is up my ass all damn day just waiting to bust me for leaving. But believe me, the minute I can get out of here and go home, you can bet your ass that's what I'm gonna do. My daughter needs me. Screw everyone else."

Walter turned to Private Lewis. "What about you? Are you going to go along with all this?" Walt stared at him, waiting for his answer.

After a moment, the boy nodded. "My mom needs me. She's all alone. As soon as I can, I'm heading back home so I can take care of her."

Walter didn't know what to think. Five days without power and the National Guard was working without pay and merely told to "contain" the problem areas with no attempt to provide assistance. Was this what their modern day humanitarian aid looked like?

He thought about the way wars were fought these days, with nameless, faceless drone strikes ordered from the comfort of the Oval Office. This was just another order. Havers was right; the president probably sat right now in an upholstered armchair in some bunker below the ground, waiting for most of America to die from starvation or kill each other.

The government never acted fast enough. Never made the tough choices quick enough. He still couldn't believe these soldiers were going to barricade people in and let them die. "Don't you all care about this country? Don't you have a sense of duty?"

Private Lewis glanced at the other man. His Adam's apple bobbed as he swallowed. "I gotta follow orders, sir."

"Damn straight. No sense in sticking your neck out for someone who doesn't give a damn about you. If we didn't have plenty of rations, it would be worse. We're already losing a few men every day. Soon it'll just be the single guys with nowhere else to go."

Walter shook his head.

He was too old to be of any use and retired long enough for no one to care about his opinions. But this whole thing boggled his mind. Barricading people inside the city instead of going in and establishing order? Keeping guardsman on duty when their families had no food or water?

This wasn't a civil war fought thousands of miles away on a continent most Americans had never visited. This was right here. Right now.

He scrubbed at his face. "Do you know for sure how far the power is out?"

A third voice answered his question. "I'm afraid that's classified."

Walter turned around. Sergeant Hickman stood a handful of steps away, his thumbs hooked in his belt. Walter gawked at him. "That's ridiculous. Whatever happened is done. It shouldn't matter who knows it."

"According to the higher-ups, it's a national security issue. Afraid I can't tell you more than that."

"Do you know if any effort is being made to provide aid? Is FEMA mobilized? What about the other branches of the military? The Marines?"

Hickman snorted. "Bet you'd like that, wouldn't you? Maybe you would get more information out of some old active-duty buddies."

Walter didn't know why the man had a bone to pick and he refused to take the bait. "I just want information. That's all. My wife and daughter are in Sacramento and I need to get home to them. I would appreciate any information you can give me."

Hickman inhaled, his nostrils flaring as he thought it over. "I can't give you any more details. But we can give you a ride. It's wheels up at 1300."

Walter stared as the staff sergeant spun on his heel and walked away.

"Somebody sure pissed in his cornflakes this morning." Havers spat another wad of crud on the ground before walking away. Only Private Lewis remained by his side.

"If I knew any more, I'd tell you, sir. But no one's said anything." He glanced at Walter with wide eyes. "That means it's bad, right?"

Walter nodded. "Yeah, kid. I'd say it's real damn bad out there." He gave the private a quick pat on the shoulder before walking toward the building where Drew still slept. They needed to pack up and get ready. In a few hours, they would be home.

CHAPTER SEVENTEEN

WALTER

Sacramento, CA
5:00 p.m.

The drive into town via a giant desert-brown convoy took hours. Walter's impatience grew with every mile. Was his family in the middle of a war zone? Were they barricaded inside the tiny bungalow while people set the rest of the city on fire? Had Madison even made it home, or was she out there somewhere, trapped and alone?

Walter ground his fist into his palm over and over as the Humvee bounced down the road. If anyone hurt his family, he wouldn't rest until he found the culprit.

"You all right?" Drew's voice snapped him out of his waking nightmare.

"Just imagining the possibilities."

"Don't do that to yourself. We'll find out soon

enough." Drew ducked to look out the window. "We're only a mile or two from my place."

"Where do you live?"

"Downtown. A little condo on N Street, about five blocks from the river."

Walter glanced at the two National Guardsmen in the front seats. "Can you all drop us off downtown? Somewhere near the Capitol?"

Both Guardsmen looked at each other before glancing in the back. "That's part of the containment area. We're headed that way, but we've got orders to lock it all down."

"What about the state government? Isn't the governor and the legislature at the Capitol?"

The man in the passenger's seat shook his head. "No. It fell yesterday. The major who came to brief us said the whole thing's on fire. The dome and everything."

The driver spoke up. "That's why we got pulled back from Portland. We've got orders to contain the violence to inside the rivers and the highways. Everything from the Sacramento and American Rivers south to Highway 50 and I-80 is going on lockdown."

Walter swallowed. "That's all of downtown."

"Midtown, too." Drew scooted forward in his seat. "My fiancée is downtown. That's where we live. I have to get to her and get her out."

"We can drop you at our checkpoint, but can't get any closer."

Walter turned to Drew. "Are you sure she's at home? You said yourself she could be anywhere."

Drew ran a hand through his shaggy hair. "I...I don't know." He glanced out the window. "But I have to get home and find out."

Walter nodded in understanding. Part of him wanted to wave as Drew set off for his place and turn in the other direction, but walking to their home from downtown would be difficult. He would never make it before dark.

What he needed was transportation. He turned to Drew. "Do you have a car?"

"Yeah. A Jetta, why?"

"Will it be at your house?"

"It should be, unless Anne took it somewhere."

Walter nodded. He could help Drew find his fiancée and they could all drive to his home in the safer, non-barricaded part of town. Walking through a riot to get to a car wasn't the best idea, but leaving Drew didn't seem right. Not when the guy had a twisted ankle and could barely walk.

"I'll go with you to your place and help you find Anne, if you'll drive me to my house when we're done."

Drew's face broke into a smile. "Thanks, Walt. That would be great."

Nothing about today was great, but Walter didn't correct him. The Humvee slowed as the driver navigated a corner and pulled into a parking lot. He put the vehicle in park and turned around to face Walter and Drew. "This is the end of the line. We're regrouping here before establishing the defensive perimeter."

Walter held out his hand. "Thanks for taking us this far."

The driver shook it. "Sorry we can't get you closer."

"It's better than the forest you found us in." Walter smiled and glanced at Drew. "Ready?"

"As ready as I'll ever be."

Walter climbed out of the Humvee and helped Drew down. Even with his ankle taped and his blisters bandaged, he still walked with a limp and at an old man's pace. They would be slow-walking ducks on the streets of downtown until they reached Drew's condo.

Walter checked his watch. "It's 5:30. We've got maybe an hour of daylight left and at least a mile to reach your place. The faster we get there, the better."

Drew nodded. "I'll do my best."

Walter grabbed both of their bags, slinging one over each shoulder. Drew needed to worry about his ankle and not his duffel. "Which way is fastest?"

Drew glanced around at the street in front of them. "North until N, then it's five blocks east."

"Let's go." Walter led the way, canvassing the street in front of them and every alley and darkened doorway they approached. Urban fighting was the worst. Besides having an endless number of places to hide, sight lines were limited. An ambush could be waiting around every brick wall or concrete pillar.

The first shop they passed had boards on the window and broken glass beyond. The second was a burned-out shell.

"This is unbelievable." Drew looked around, eyes wide. "Why do people riot when the power goes out? It makes no sense. Do they want to live in chaos?"

"Mobs have a life of their own." Walter glanced

around and hitched the bags higher up on his shoulders. He picked up the pace a bit, willing Drew to walk faster. "Once something happens and the fuse is lit, the hive mentality takes over. Everyone is anonymous and part of this larger collective. It's intoxicating."

"You sound like you like them."

Walter shook his head. "No. But I understand them. Ever been to a live sporting event like a college basketball or football game?"

Drew nodded.

"It's the same sort of feeling you get when the crowd is cheering and the team is playing great, only times a thousand. The mob is running on endorphins. It's a chance to strike back at the government, the police, anyone and everything."

He thought back to the LA riots. Days of unfettered chaos that seemed to go on forever. "How old were you in 1992?"

Drew counted back. "Eight. Why?"

Walter snorted. "I was twenty-one and I'd just gone to Los Angeles to celebrate when the riots broke out."

Drew hesitated. "You were there?"

"Yep. At a bar. The whole twenty-one-shot challenge." Walter smiled. "I was young and stupid."

"Were you caught up in the riot? How did you survive?"

Walter would never forget the sounds of the city that night. "It was chaos. I watched looters smash a storefront across the street and barge in while a cop car rolled right by, doing nothing."

"Seriously?"

Walter nodded. "The bar we were in was a total dive. It had these metal accordion gates the owner could pull shut and lock, so he did that right away. After that, we helped him cover the windows with all the furniture in the place and we spent the rest of the night behind the bar taking turns with the shotgun he kept under the top."

Drew shook his head. "I remember my parents talking about it and some teachers in school but I didn't know it was that bad."

"It was worse. People shooting other people for no reason. Setting fire to buildings. Tipping cars. Looting. You name it, they did it. Eleven thousand people were arrested. And that was over a jury verdict, not the end of the modern world."

"How did you get out?"

"Eventually the crowds moved on from that area and we left."

Drew waved his arms about. "Are they really going to barricade this whole area in? It doesn't look so bad here. Sure these buildings have damage, but I don't see anyone out on the streets now. Maybe it all died out."

Walter frowned. "They wouldn't be setting up a defense if it wasn't still raging. From the looks of it, this part of the city has already been picked clean. The mob will have moved on to somewhere new."

Walter motioned around. "When we walked out of the bar in '92, it looked a lot like this."

Which meant danger lurked around every corner.

Drew fell silent as the pair trudged down the street. Walter attempted to rein in his impatience while Drew struggled to put weight on his foot. Every block brought them closer to destruction. A burned-out cop car. A mailbox ripped from the ground stuck out a second-floor window. A building with nothing left but scorched beams and blackened rubble.

Five days. The amount of destruction in five days was unbelievable. With the National Guard not coming in to restore order, but merely to barricade the violence in, it would only get worse. People would become desperate.

Deadly.

They neared N Street and an explosion caught Walter off guard. A building several blocks away erupted in a cloud of smoke. "I think we've found the edge of the riot."

Drew's eyes went wide. "That's right by my place."

Walter nodded. They would need to brave the violence to reach his fiancée. "You ready for this?"

"Do I have a choice?"

"Not if you want to find Anne."

Drew closed his eyes for a moment. "Listen. If I don't make it—"

Walter held up his hand. "None of that fatalist bullshit. You'll make it." Walter motioned toward the street. "I'll lead."

CHAPTER EIGHTEEN

MADISON

Sloane Residence
    7:00 p.m.

An entire day had passed and they were still going around in circles over the man tied up in the master bedroom.

"We need to talk to him and assess the threat."

Madison wrapped her arms around herself. As soon as the sun set, the temperature inside the house dropped ten degrees. They would get through the summer all right without power, but how would they survive the winter?

The more she thought about the future, the more it scared her. It was easier to focus on getting home or getting supplies. One task to accomplish or mission to complete. When her mind wandered, she shut down.

She glanced up at her mom. "You sound like Dad."

A week ago, her mom would never have talked about a person as a threat or contemplated the use of force to obtain information. Now she leaned back on the kitchen counter, tactical pants bulging with extra magazines and a pistol shoved in her belt.

Madison missed her old mom. The one who baked muffins and hugged her good morning and never, ever saw the bad in people first.

"Your mom is right." Brianna pulled her hair into a tight bun on top of her head. "We need to get it done. He needs to eat and drink and go to the bathroom. Now's a good time to ask him some questions. Starvation's a good motivator."

"I can't believe we're having this conversation."

"You're the one who tied him up."

Madison glared at Brianna. "What else was I supposed to do?"

"You could have used Wanda's gun to finish him off. It would have saved us a lot of trouble."

"That's enough." Madison's mom pushed off the counter. "No one is killing anyone unless it's in self-defense."

"He attacked us. He broke in. I'd say anything we do to him *is* self-defense."

"Not according to the law, it isn't."

Brianna threw up her hands. "Who cares about the law? It's not like we have a country or a state anymore."

"Of course we do."

"Then where is it? I haven't seen a single aid truck or police car or military vehicle drive by since this whole thing started, have you?"

Peyton spoke up. "There was the one cop we ran into."

Brianna scoffed. "Mr. Dudley Do-Right? He doesn't count." She shook her head. "He's probably rotting somewhere near that park right now, his corpse half-eaten by——"

"Don't be gross."

Brianna turned on Madison. "I'm not being gross, I'm being realistic. While all of you sit around here with your thumbs up your butts trying to drum up the courage to do what needs to be done, someone out there is plotting a way to kill all of us and take our supplies."

Madison's temper flared. "You don't know that."

"It's what I would do." Brianna pointed toward the bedroom where the man was held prisoner. "It's what he was doing. Don't be naïve. It's survival of the fittest now and I'm not weak."

Madison's mom held up her hands. "No one is saying you're weak, Brianna. You've demonstrated time and again that you're more than capable of handling yourself. But we need to be rational about this."

Brianna scowled, but didn't respond.

"The more information we can get out of him, the more prepared we will be." Tracy clapped her hands. "Enough talking. I'm going in. Who wants to cover me?"

Brianna began to speak, but Peyton cut her off. "I'll do it."

All the heads in the room turned his way. "Are you sure?"

Peyton nodded. "It's about time I pulled my own

weight. And I'm the biggest. I figure even if I don't shoot him, I can at least intimidate him."

Madison's mom glanced around. "Any objections?" When no one spoke up, she continued. "All right, then. Madison, you and Brianna take up watch in the front and back. Tucker, you stay in the living room with Wanda. If he tries to escape or do something stupid, we'll need back up."

Tucker grabbed a shotgun and stood up. "Will do, Mrs. Sloane."

"Peyton, you're coming with me."

Madison watched her mom and her best friend file out of the kitchen and head toward the master bedroom. She wished she could be there as well, but her mom was right. Someone needed to stand guard over not just the house, but Brianna's fiery temper.

She was a loose cannon at the moment; so charged up over a potential threat and escaping the Walmart that she'd lost all common sense. Madison paused. Unless Brianna was right.

Brianna's parents had prepared her for this exact situation: the end of the modern world. Whether it came by nuclear war or a cyber attack or their very own sun, Brianna was equipped to handle it.

Madison and her mom and the rest of them were still trying to figure it out. She glanced at the quiet hall and picked up one of the new handguns Brianna had stolen from Walmart.

Hopefully she wouldn't have to use it.

CHAPTER NINETEEN

TRACY

7:30 p.m.

"I HOPE YOU'RE NOT SQUEAMISH." T RACY GLANCED AT
Peyton as she opened the door to the master bedroom.

"I'll be fine."

"Good. Because I'm going to need your help." She
eased inside and took stock of the situation. The man
Madison had tied up groaned and shifted position,
tugging on his taped arms.

With his mouth taped shut, all he could do was
mumble obscenities, but that was about to change.
Tracy didn't know how her husband did it. He had
deployed multiple times over his twenty years on active
duty. Every deployment she worried. Would his plane be
shot down? Would he be captured?

She pictured him like this, tied to a post, unable to

eat or sleep or go to the bathroom until someone let him. Every time, Walter had come home. He'd never been injured, never been shot out of the sky, never taken prisoner.

He would make it home this time, too. She had to have faith. But until then, she was in charge.

Tracy crouched in front of the man. "I'm sorry. This is going to hurt." She reached for the tape across his mouth and tugged at a little corner. As soon as she gripped enough to do the job, she pulled.

The tape came off with a grunt of pain from the man. "About damn time. How about you get this rope off me, too?"

"Sorry. I can't do that." Tracy stood up. "I'm going to need to ask you some questions first."

The man snorted. "Good luck, lady. I'm not tellin' you nothin'."

"How badly do you need to piss?"

The man shifted on the floor.

"Or eat or have some nice, refreshing water?" Tracy held up a brand-new bottle of water. "I bet you're dying for a sip."

She unscrewed the cap. "Want some?"

The man wavered. "What do you want?"

"I want to know why you came here, what you hoped to accomplish, and who else is involved."

"Then you'll give me some water?"

She smiled. "I might even let you go."

His shoulders slumped, and the man hung his head. The dried blood from the wound had crusted into his hair in a brown, chunky mess. "Bill is going to kill me."

Tracy steeled herself. "Bill put you up to this? Bill Donovan?"

The man looked up with a nod. "Yeah. He said you guys had a ton of food and water and that no one was watching the place. All I had to do was sneak in and grab a case or two. You'd never miss it."

Tracy glanced at Peyton. "That makes no sense. Bill knows we're armed. I stuck a gun in his face for goodness' sake."

The hostage's eyes went wide. "He told me you didn't have any weapons. That it was just a bunch of women and kids."

"That doesn't mean we aren't capable of defending ourselves."

"Obviously."

Tracy bent down and offered the man some water, holding it while he drank a few sips. "I'm Tracy Sloane."

"Russell Unders. I'd shake your hand, but I'm kind of tied up."

Tracy stood up and tried not to laugh. "I hate to tell you this, Russell, but Bill lied to you. About a lot of things."

"I'm beginning to figure that out."

Tracy turned to Peyton. "Can you spare a shirt for Russell here? We can let him go and get him cleaned up and something to eat."

"You really think that's a good idea?"

Tracy wasn't one hundred percent sure, but Russell seemed like a good man. If he'd wanted to hurt them when he broke in, he could have. Instead of sneaking into the bedroom, he could have shot at anyone through the window. Or organized a party to come break the door down.

If he told the truth, Tracy needed to worry about Bill Donovan, not Russell Unders. She nodded at Peyton. "I do. Find the scissors too, so we can cut him loose."

Peyton opened the bedroom door and stepped out into the hall. Before the door shut behind him, she heard Brianna shout.

"We've got visitors!"

Tracy glanced at Russell before turning toward the open door. She shouted at Peyton as he ran toward the living room. "Who is it? What's going on?"

After a moment, Peyton shouted back. "Get ready! I think it's an ambush."

Oh, no. Tracy pulled her handgun out of her waistband. They weren't prepared to defend an attack. She glanced at Russell. "Could these be friends of yours coming to rescue you?"

He shrugged. "I don't know. If you let me go, I can help. If it's someone I know, I can diffuse the situation, maybe get them to stand down."

Tracy frowned. She had planned on letting him go, but not with a threat looming outside. "I'm sorry, I can't let you go. Not now."

He struggled against his ropes. "I can help. I won't hurt you or anyone in the house."

Tracy stepped toward the door.

"You can't leave me here! What if the people breaking in don't know me? They could be thugs from another part of town. Come on, I'll be a sitting duck!"

Tracy exhaled. "I'm sorry. But I can't." Before Russell could say another word in his defense, Tracy slipped out and shut the door behind her.

She could hear his shouts for help, but she ignored them. If they made it out of this ambush alive, she could reassess the situation. If not, letting him go wouldn't do any good.

With a deep breath, she hustled into the chaos of the rest of the house.

CHAPTER TWENTY

MADISON

"It's too dark. I can't see anything." Madison squinted in an effort to see past the kitchen window and into the backyard. There could have been fifty people all crowded in between the fence and the patio and she would never have known. "We need to throw a glow stick out there or something so we can see!"

"And tell whoever is out there exactly where we are? Not a chance." Tucker crouched down next to Madison, a rifle from Walmart in his hand. Thanks to Brianna's quick thinking as she fled the store with Madison's mom and Tucker, they had a gun for every person in the house and a bit of ammo.

It wasn't enough for a firefight, but it might make whoever was out there think twice about breaking in.

"We need to stay low and concealed. If someone tries to break in, we shoot. That's all there is to it." With a ball cap on backward to keep his shaggy hair out of his face and a black sweatshirt covering his limbs, Tucker could almost pass for a jock instead of a science geek.

"Easy for you to say. A lot harder to do."

"What other choice do we have? We don't have enough ammo to engage. What if whoever is out there has guns, too?" Tucker frowned. "Someone could die, Madison."

"We're all going to die if we don't do something." Brianna crouched down next to Tucker, the butt of her shotgun tight against her shoulder. "What are you doing here? Shouldn't you be in the front?"

"Mrs. Sloane and Peyton are there now."

Madison turned to Tucker. "Did the guy in the bedroom tell them anything? Do they know what's going on?"

"Supposedly he's harmless, but your mom won't let him go with all this going on. She's got the front covered. We're supposed to keep anyone from coming in the back."

"What about the bedrooms?"

Brianna rolled her eyes. "Wanda is standing guard."

Tucker groaned. "She'll get us killed. I'm going back there."

Madison touched his arm. "I can go. You can stay here with Brianna if you want."

"No. Let me handle Wanda. For some reason she listens to me."

Brianna leaned in. "It's the greasy hair and the River Cats hat. They make all the ladies swoon."

Tucker gave his girlfriend a quick kiss on the cheek. "Be careful."

"You, too."

As soon as Tucker was out of earshot, Madison spoke up. "Do you really think Wanda is a liability?"

"One hundred percent. But so is that guy tied up in the bedroom. Between the two of them, they're liable to ruin everything."

Madison stared at the sliding glass door, willing her vision to improve. "I hope you're wrong."

"So do I." Brianna slid to the side while still in a crouch, easing past the edge of the table to get a better view. As she did so, shots rang out in the front of the house. "Shit!" She ducked back where Madison still hid and grabbed the edge of the table.

"What are you doing?"

"Help me flip it! We need cover!" Madison grabbed the table with both hands and pulled. It barely budged.

"It's too heavy! We can't lift it."

Brianna cursed and slung her shotgun over her shoulder. "Grab the edge again. I'm going around to flip it."

"No! You'll be exposed."

"We'll be dead if I don't."

Before Madison could say another word, Brianna raced around the side of the table and crouched beneath it. "Ready? Pull!"

With Madison pulling and Brianna pushing, the heavy wood table lifted and wobbled and finally fell over with a crash. The handful of things sitting on the top fell to the floor as Brianna rushed back around.

Another round of gunfire erupted from the front of the house.

"What's going on?"

"I don't know. It sounds like they're trying to come in the front."

"The entertainment center is in the way."

"Maybe it's a diversion. We need to be ready." Brianna set the barrel of her gun up on the edge of the table and Madison did the same. If anyone tried to come in through the kitchen, he or she would be dead as soon as they broke the glass.

Madison's mom called out from the other room. "Is everyone all right?"

Brianna answered first. "We're fine in the kitchen."

"No activity in the hall." Tucker sounded calm and confident.

Madison asked about her mom. "Are you okay?"

"They shot out the front window, but the entertainment center stopped them. I don't know where they are, but be ready. They haven't given up."

Shifting her position behind the table, Madison counted the shells they had in reserve. All three shotguns in the house—the two Madison and Brianna held and the one Peyton took to the living room—were partially loaded to the max with five each, and based on her hasty count, they had fourteen left in their box. Peyton couldn't have many more.

Tucker had a rifle and a box of ammo. Her mom had a handgun, two extra magazines, and at least fifty rounds thanks to Brianna. They might be able to hold off an attack, but for how long?

She focused on the window. Every shot would have to count. Her heart slammed against her chest, every breath speeding it up until she felt like a racehorse about to be released from the chute. Something was coming. Madison could feel it.

All at once gunfire erupted. Brianna jumped up. "It's from the hall. Tucker!" She turned to Madison. "Cover me!"

"What? No! Brianna—"

Before Madison could say another word, Brianna jumped out from behind the table and raced toward the hallway. Madison held up her shotgun, unable to see into the backyard to give her roommate the protection she needed.

Every step seemed to take an hour as Madison willed Brianna to make it past the window and down the hall to help Tucker and Wanda. *Come on. Come on.* Madison gripped the shotgun tight to her shoulder, finger on the trigger.

When the glass of the sliding door splintered, she didn't hesitate. Madison shot.

Boom!

The gun recoiled hard and fast, the barrel flying up into the air as the sliding glass door shattered into a million little pieces and dropped to the floor. Her ears rang, drowning out the shouts and screams from the other room.

Madison brought the gun back against her shoulder and shot again.

Boom!

Smoke and the scent of cordite filled the air. The empty shell hit the floor and Madison fired again.

Boom!

She didn't know if Brianna made it. Had she been hit? Was she lying on the floor ten feet away, sucking in her last breath? Madison gripped the gun tighter and waited with her head barely visible above the table.

When had breathing become so hard? She labored with each inhale, struggling to get enough oxygen. Her heart beat like she'd run a marathon and the sweat on her palms made it hard to grip the gun.

"Mom! Brianna! Tucker!"

She still couldn't hear. Were they okay? Should she move? Fear slinked down her spine, nasty slivers jabbing her like knives.

People were breaking in and trying to destroy everything they worked for. Everything they saved and risked their lives over. Everything that was supposed to keep them alive.

The more she thought about it, the angrier she became. The mini-mart where they risked getting shot to grab more food and water and maps to get them home. The Walmart where her mom and Brianna and Tucker could have died.

Brianna and Tucker had delayed going to Truckee to keep them safe, and now they were getting shot at here. If Brianna died, how would she tell her parents? Madison didn't even know where the cabin was located.

She ground her palm against her temple. Fear didn't rule her. She wasn't going to crouch there behind the table while her mom and friends battled for their lives. Madison unloaded the rest of the shotgun out the broken door before reloading. A handful of shells went into in her pockets.

Screw waiting and being safe. She was going to protect her house and her family whatever the cost. She stood up and fired into the dark cavern of the backyard. Three steps around the table and she fired again. Another four as she ran toward the hall.

The second Madison cleared the door, she stopped, back against the wall. Brianna wasn't in view. She rushed into the living room and stumbled to a stop.

The couch had been flipped over and Peyton crouched behind it. Her mom and Brianna were nowhere to be found. "Are you all right?" Madison slid down to where Peyton half-sat.

"Yeah." Sweat poured down his face and he dragged in labored breaths.

"Where is everyone?"

"The bedrooms." Madison started to move when Peyton grabbed her arm. "It's bad, Madison. Wanda got shot. Maybe Tucker, too. You might want to stay out here."

Madison shook him off. "No! I need to go. What if they need help?"

"Who's going to protect them from this direction? Just me?" Peyton glanced down at his gun. "I've got two shells left. That's it."

This can't be happening. Madison glanced at the dark hall then back at Peyton. However much she wanted to help, Peyton was right. She needed to stay. She slid down to sit next to him and fished in her pocket.

"Here. I've got a few more shells. We can split them."

Peyton wrapped his hand around hers before she pulled away. "Thanks."

"Don't thank me yet." She focused on the way she'd come. "We still need to get out of this alive."

CHAPTER TWENTY-ONE

WALTER

Downtown Sacramento
5:30 p.m.

"Holy shit." Drew pulled back from the edge of the building, his cheeks paling more by the second. "We'll never make it. It's a war zone out there."

Walter believed it. From the shouts and the crashes and the intermittent gunfire, it sounded just like Los Angeles all those years ago. He exhaled. They could turn back, hike to the command center set up by the National Guard, and leave Drew's fiancée in the midst of all this chaos.

Or they could man up and do the right thing.

Walter scrubbed at his face. "How badly do you want to see Anne?"

Drew didn't hesitate. "More than anything."

"Then we don't have a choice."

"Don't come with me."

Walter balked. "What are you talking about? Of course I'm going."

Drew shook his head. "I mean it. You have a family, Walt. You should be putting them first. Anne is my responsibility, not yours."

Walter glanced down at Drew's taped ankle. "I'm not leaving you here. That's a death sentence."

His former co-pilot puffed up his chest. "I can do it."

"It'll be easier with two of us."

Drew nodded. "Yes, it will. But I can't ask you to risk your life. Not for me."

"I'm not doing it for you. I doing it to help your fiancée. Besides, I need a car."

Drew cracked a small grin. "Are you using me just to get access to a vehicle?"

"Maybe." Walter clapped Drew on the back. "Come on. The daylight's waning."

Walter advanced toward the street, glancing behind him to make sure they could retreat if necessary. As he exhaled, eased around the corner.

Drew was wrong.

War zone didn't come close to describing the chaos. Burned-out buildings. Fires still raging. A car crash in the middle of the intersection. A dead body lying ten feet away.

Christ.

Walter motioned for Drew to follow. Staying close to the buildings, they navigated over broken glass and sheets of plywood, dropped radios and smashed televisions. The drugstore on the corner had been looted and burned, shelves along the far walls the only thing left standing inside.

Drew hobbled behind Walter, intermittently cursing and grabbing the wall for support as his ankle gave him trouble. They didn't have time to rest. The sooner they made it to safety the better.

A person appeared in the broken window of a shop half a block down and Walter rushed Drew into an alcove. The man wore a white T-shirt streaked with soot and blood and he held a baseball bat in one hand.

"What's happening?"

Walter shushed Drew and pressed further back into the shadows. Maybe they should have waited until nightfall, but then how would they leave? The National Guard would erect the barricades and Walter, Drew, and Anne would be trapped.

His family would fear the worst if they didn't already.

He leaned forward to survey the street. The man with the bat was gone. "Let's go."

They crept back out onto the sidewalk, fast walking toward the corner, when a whoop and a crash made Walter duck. The windows to a tax preparer's office across the street shattered. Drew jumped behind him.

Seconds later the scent of smoke assaulted Walter's nose and flames leapt out the front of the store.

"What happened?"

"Molotov cocktail, I'd guess. Come on." Walter motioned for Drew to keep going. They reached the intersection and raced across with Walter holding onto

Drew's arm to keep him upright. "How many more blocks?"

Drew glanced at the street sign. "Two and a half. My building is on the right."

"Can you run?"

"I can try."

Walter took off at a loping pace, hoping Drew could keep up. Only two more blocks.

A series of shouts rang out from somewhere to their left followed by a volley of gunfire. They couldn't stop. They were so close.

Walter glanced behind him. Drew lagged about ten feet behind. He didn't wait for him.

At the next intersection, a fire raged, burning what looked to have been a restaurant, the flames licking the second-floor windows of apartments above. As Walter dodged the heat, Drew called out.

"Walter! I need to stop. I can't—"

Walter spun around. Drew clutched a light post, wincing as he lifted his foot off the ground. Walter wanted to scream at him. He needed to suck it up and find a way. They would be killed if they stayed in one place.

Moving was the only chance they had. He rushed back to him. "You have to move. I don't care if you never walk again after this. If we don't go, we'll die."

Walter wrapped his arm around Drew's back and helped him off the light post. He already carried both bags and now he shouldered Drew's weight. *So be it.*

He half-dragged, half-carried Drew past the burning building and fell into an alcove just beyond.

The brick walls sheltered them from the worst of the heat and stairs led up to a second floor with a door at the top.

Leaning Drew back on the wall, Walter sucked in some much-needed air. Sweat soaked his shirt, his back and shoulders ached from carrying the bags and dragging Drew, and he couldn't catch his breath.

But he wasn't a quitter. "We're getting you to your condo, Drew. Whatever it takes."

Drew grimaced. "It's still a block away. The noise is louder up ahead. I think we're running into the mob."

"We'll make it. We just need to push a little harder. Dig a little deeper."

After a moment, Drew nodded. "All right. Just give me a minute to catch my breath."

Walter would have given anything for a gun. Just to hold one in his hand. His old service pistol would be perfect, but he'd settle for a POS revolver. Anything to give them an advantage. But a loaded gun wasn't about to fall from the sky or appear at his feet.

They were doing this unarmed and injured.

He pushed off the wall. "Come on. We've rested enough." Walter eased toward the corner and stuck his head out enough to see. Another intersection and Drew's building should be in the middle of the block.

Three hundred yards at most. They would make it. They had to. He motioned forward. "Let's go."

The rest of the block passed by in record time, Drew kept up beside him, and they managed to pass three buildings without incident.

Maybe that's why he didn't scope out the

intersection before they rushed into it. Or maybe it was the joy of Drew pointing out his building. So close!

He never saw the bullet coming. Drew fell in front of him, arms flailing, chest slamming into the asphalt.

Walter whipped around. A man with a bandana around his face and a hat low over his eyes stood beside a car, holding a rifle up in the air like he'd won a heavyweight fight. Another man across the street shouted in encouragement.

Shit. Walter scooped Drew up, hands digging under his armpits and dragged, just like he had done on so many CFTs. Backpedaling, he made it across the intersection and dove behind the edge of the closest building before the next shot rang out.

Shouts followed.

In seconds they would be upon them. Walter glanced around in a panic. The restaurant had burned, but not completely. He dragged Drew through the debris, around overturned tables and broken chairs, avoiding the glass and twisted metal as best he could. One piece cut his jeans and dug into his leg, but he ignored it.

Walter ducked into the kitchen as the voices grew louder.

He pulled up behind the prep counter and metal cabinets and flipped Drew over. *Oh, God.* Blood bloomed across Drew's T-shirt from a gunshot to the shoulder. He searched for a pulse. Faint, but steady. If he could get him somewhere safe…

"Drew! Drew, wake up! I need you buddy." Walter smacked Drew across the face. "Wake up!"

Drew groaned and bobbed his head. "W-What happened?"

"You've been shot. The guys who did it are closing in. Is there another way into your building instead of the front?"

Drew moaned. "Uh… yeah. The alley. Beside the restaurant. The key's in my… pocket."

Walter shoved his hand in Drew's pockets, fumbling around for the key. His fingers scraped metal and he wrapped his hand around the keychain before pulling it free. He gripped the keys so tight, they cut into his palm. *Okay. I can do this.*

Grabbing Drew under the arm, Walter supported his weight as he navigated through the kitchen toward the door with an exit sign above it. They could still make it.

He pushed the door open as a commotion picked up in the restaurant. The men from the street were inside.

Please don't find us. Walter dragged Drew through the door and caught it before it slammed. He let it close as quietly as possible before turning to face the alley. Drew's condo building. *It must be.*

He tugged Drew toward a metal perforated door to the first-floor garage, propping him up on the side of the building as he searched through the keys. The first one did nothing. The second wouldn't even fit in the lock.

The third was a car key. The fourth… *Please God, be this one.* The fourth turned in the lock. Walter sent up a silent prayer and grabbed Drew, tugging him inside as the door to the restaurant slammed open.

He ducked behind the wall to the garage and let the metal door close, hoping like hell it locked automatically. As he dragged Drew down the hall toward the stairs, the door handle shook and the men outside shouted.

They couldn't get in. Another volley of gunfire erupted, but it wouldn't do any good. Walter had done it. He'd gotten them inside Drew's condo building.

Now he just needed to save Drew's life.

CHAPTER TWENTY-TWO

MADISON

S LOANE R ESIDENCE
9:00 p.m.

"W HERE ARE THEY?" M ADISON COULD BARELY contain her impatience. At least twenty minutes had passed since the last shot from either inside or outside.

"I don't know." Peyton shifted position behind the couch and risked a glance toward the kitchen.

"We can't wait anymore. We need to see if anyone needs help."

Peyton exhaled. "You go. We can't leave the whole house exposed."

Madison reached out and gave his arm a squeeze. "Thanks." Before Peyton could respond, Madison jumped up and rushed down the hall. She reached the master bedroom and turned the knob.

As the door swung open, she raised her gun, but

there was no need. The room was empty. No mom, no friends, and no guy tied up to the end of the bed. The board Peyton had nailed to the broken window dangled broken and loose off one side.

Whoever shot at the house had rescued the captured man. Did that mean they were gone? Was it over?

She backed out of the room and shut the door before approaching her bedroom. A faint light shone from under the door. With a light tap of her knuckles, Madison knocked. "It's Madison. Let me in."

The door unlocked and swung open. Brianna stood beside it, eyes wide and haunted. "What's going on out there? It's too quiet."

Madison shrugged. "Nothing."

"Where's Peyton?"

"Keeping watch."

Madison's mom called out from the other side of the bed. "Tell him to come in here. We need to make a plan."

From her vantage point, Madison couldn't see much more than the top of her mom's head. The lantern sitting on the side table cast half of the room in shadow. Was her mom hurt? Did someone die?

She frowned. "What about keeping watch?"

"I think whoever did this is gone. They got what they wanted."

"The man we caught?"

Brianna nodded. "He's what they were after."

Madison stepped back and retraced her steps before calling Peyton to follow. When they both squeezed into the tiny room, Brianna shut and locked the door. As

Madison walked around the edge of the bed, she gasped.

Wanda lay on the floor, unconscious. Tucker kneeled beside her, his hands pressed down over a blood-soaked ball of fabric wadded up against her pelvis. He grimaced as Madison approached. "Sorry. We used some of your clothes."

"It's okay." Madison crouched down beside the woman. In her unconscious state, Wanda's wrinkles smoothed and she could imagine what she looked like at half her age when she was young and carefree. "Is she okay?"

"No." Her mom stood up and wiped at her forehead with a hand stained in blood. "She's been shot in the lower abdomen. We can't get the bleeding to stop."

"She needs to go to a hospital!"

Brianna spoke up. "The only trauma center in the area is the UC Davis Medical Center. It's downtown."

"So? We go there."

"No." Her mom shook her head. "Downtown isn't safe. When Wanda and I were at her apartment, a man there said downtown was engulfed in riots. We can't risk it. Besides, what could the hospital do for her? There's no power."

"But there are nurses and doctors. Someone can do something."

Tucker chimed in. "No, they can't. All the blood stored is bad by now. Surgical equipment isn't sanitary. If riots are in the area, they've probably already been looted for all of the painkillers and antibiotics."

He shifted position, glancing down at Wanda's wound. "Besides, I don't think she's going to make it."

Madison stared at Tucker's bloody hands. *This can't be happening.* "How did she get shot?"

"It was a coordinated attack. After they shot out the picture window in the living room, they shot out the sliding glass door out back. But that was all a distraction."

Madison frowned at her mom. "What do you mean?"

"While we were busy defending the house, someone else broke through the plywood covering the window."

"In the master?"

Tucker nodded. "By the time I got back here, it was too late. Two guys were cutting the ropes off the man and Wanda was lying on the floor in a heap. Blood was pumping out of her and..." He shook his head. "I've never seen anything like it."

"What happened to the men?"

"They took the other guy and left through the window."

"Did they try to shoot you?"

"No. When I busted in, one pointed a pistol at me, but I held up my hands and told him I just wanted to help Wanda. The guy we'd tied up told the other one to let me, so he did."

"If it weren't for Tucker, she'd be dead already." Madison's mom rubbed the back of her neck. "He's slowed the bleeding, but there's too much internal bleeding. The bullet is still in there somewhere."

Her mom shook her head. "That guy you tied up

seemed so nice. We were about to let him go when the shooting started."

"Do you think he was lying?"

"I don't know."

Madison exhaled. She couldn't believe it. Earlier that day, they were all standing around, laughing and joking. Wanda rigged up the shower and they all managed to clean themselves up. She had even talked about setting up a laundry station and coming up with a way to use scraps from meals to keep Fireball alive.

She glanced around. "Has anyone seen the cat?"

"Wanda's about to die and you're asking about a cat?" Brianna eyed her like she she'd gotten a head injury.

"Wanda loves that cat. We need to keep him safe. It's what she would want."

"She's not dead yet." Peyton's brows knit together as he stared at her still form. "Let's not talk about her like she is."

Madison's mom nodded. "We'll stay here until she either stabilizes or… doesn't make it. Then we'll make a decision."

"What do you mean?" Madison glanced around at everyone in the room. "Why wouldn't we stay here?"

Brianna scoffed. "All of the windows are shot out. Someone tried to kill us."

"No." Peyton disagreed. "They came to get one of their own. If we had let him go in the beginning…"

"I did what I thought was best at the time. I didn't know he would have friends or that they would come for him." Madison balled her hands into fists. "I thought if we let him leave, that for sure he would come back and try to rob us again."

"We should have killed him when we had the chance." Brianna crossed her arms over her chest. "Now he's out there, angry and hurt, and he knows what we've got. We're sitting ducks."

Madison couldn't believe what she was hearing. "You're talking about murder, Brianna."

"What does it matter? No one's going to punish us. It's survival of the fittest now. I'm not going to be a sitting duck."

"You really think after all this, he's going to come back?"

"Of course. That's what they do. Looters and moochers take and take until there's nothing left and then they move on." She pointed at the master bedroom. "All the food and water was stashed in there, Madison. He's seen everything. He won't stop and neither will his friends until they get what they're after."

"And what's that?"

"Everything we have."

Madison reeled. A few days ago Brianna had been this carefree, bubbly teenager with a million curls and the energy to match. Now she stood there like a post-apocalyptic warrior, shotgun slung over her shoulder and a scowl on her face.

The rest of her friends weren't that far off. Tucker was covered in Wanda's blood and leaning over her as he pressed down on her wound. Peyton had dark circles under his eyes and the scruffy beginnings of a beard. And her mom…

Madison glanced up at her. She looked bone-tired, but determined, too. "What do you think we should do?"

As her mom opened her mouth to respond, Tucker interrupted. "Hey guys?"

"Yeah?"

"I think…" Tucker leaned back on his heels and removed his hands from Wanda's body. "I think she's gone."

Madison's mom rushed to Wanda's side and placed her fingers on her throat. After a moment, she lowered her head. "Tucker's right. Wanda's dead."

Oh, no. Madison covered her mouth with her hand. "This is all my fault. If I hadn't tied him up, if I hadn't insisted we not kill him or let him go…" She trailed off, rage and despair rising inside her like boats on a wave of tears.

They slipped down her cheeks and blurred her vision and Madison crumpled onto the bed. Sobs racked her body.

A hand landed softly on her back, rubbing up and down. "It's not your fault, Madison." Brianna's words were gentle, but firm. "You didn't tell her to hit him over the head or barricade herself in the bedroom. She did that all on her own."

"But I'm the reason he was still here. I'm the reason his friends broke in."

Her mom reached up and grabbed her hand, squeezing as she talked. "There's nothing you can do about it now. Wanda is gone and we need to honor her.

Not wallow in what-ifs. She would want us to persevere, not fall apart."

Madison snorted back snot and nodded. "I still feel responsible."

"We're all responsible, even Wanda."

Peyton pushed off the wall where he had been leaning. "Do you all have a shovel? We should bury her."

Madison's mom nodded. "In the garage. But let's wait until morning. She can rest here until then."

It was too real. Too raw and painful. Madison stood up and rushed from the room, blinking back another wave of tears as she stumbled down the hall. As she neared the kitchen, she paused.

What is that? She snorted again, clearing her nose of wet and sticky grief. She made her way toward the smell, past the tipped-over couch, and into the kitchen.

Every step the smell increased, thickening and turning pungent. She rounded the corner and froze. *Oh, no. It can't be. They couldn't have...*

She turned and cupped her hands around her mouth before she screamed. "FIRE! FIRE!"

CHAPTER TWENTY-THREE

TRACY

Sloane Residence
   10:30 p.m.

Madison's scream echoed through the bedroom. "Fire!"

Tracy jumped up, nearly tripping over Wanda's dead body as she rushed toward her daughter. The second she entered the hall, she smelled the smoke. It hung close to the ceiling and Tracy ducked to make it through without inhaling too much.

Bringing the hem of her shirt up to cover her nose and mouth, Tracy made it into the kitchen. The flames licked across the back wall of the house, rising higher faster than Tracy could process. From below the wood chair rail to above in seconds, to across the butcher block counter and onto the cafe curtains above the sink.

Her house was burning. They would lose it all.

Smoke and fear tightened her chest and Tracy rushed toward her daughter who fruitlessly threw their precious water on the flames. She grabbed Madison's arms.

"Stop! Honey, stop! It's no use."

"Mom, we can put it out. We can contain it." Madison struggled in her mother's grip.

"No, Madison. We can't. It's too big."

Her daughter lunged away from her, dangerously close to the scalding heat. "We just lost Wanda, we can't lose the house, too!" She grabbed another trash can and threw the contents at the flames.

They hissed and popped and surged higher.

She had to see it was pointless. "You can't stop it, Madison!"

"I can try."

Peyton rushed up, the flames reflected in his wide eyes. He turned to Tracy. "What do we do?"

"Get everyone together. We need to secure as many supplies as we can. Pull the cars onto the road and load them up. Backpacks, sleeping bags, all the guns and ammo. And food. As much food and water as you can carry. Quick."

"What about her?" He pointed at Madison.

"I'll handle my daughter. Go."

Peyton ran off and Tracy turned back to Madison. Despite the heat, tears surged down Madison's face as she took off her jacket and used it to bat at the flames.

If she kept this up, she would get herself killed. Tracy lunged for her, wrapping her arms around Madison's middle and dragging her back, away from the flames. She shoved her against the far wall. "Stop!"

"No!" Madison screamed in her face. "We have to save it!"

"It's gone! We need to save ourselves." Tracy reached out and put her hands on Madison's shoulders. "Go help your friends load the food and water and supplies into the cars."

"But the house…" Madison choked on the smoke and her own snot. "Dad won't know where to find us if we don't have a house." She fell into Tracy's arms as the last words came out and all Tracy could do was hug her daughter for a moment.

"We can talk about it later. But right now, we need to move." She pulled back and took her daughter's face in her hands. "Help your friends, Madison. Please."

At last, her daughter nodded and took off for the master bedroom where the majority of the supplies were located.

Tracy exhaled and took one last look at the kitchen she'd so lovingly renovated only a few years before. They were supposed to make so many memories in this house. It was supposed to last the rest of their lives.

Now a fire turned the pale blue paint to ash and the kitchen table to kindling. She backed up away from the heat, and turned around. Damn the people who did this. Damn Bill and his selfish ways. If she didn't have an example to set for her daughter…

No. This would hurt, but it wouldn't wreck them. No matter what, Tracy would find a way to survive.

She rushed down the hall and into the bedroom. Peyton and Brianna were taking turns throwing cases of water and Gatorade and boxes of packaged food out of the broken window and into the backyard.

"Let me help." Tracy ran up and joined in, tossing boxes of granola bars and toilet paper out the window. "Peyton, you go around back and help load the cars. I can handle this."

"Will do." Peyton hustled off and Tracy and Brianna worked into a rhythm, one throwing while one bent to pick up another case.

"How much of this do you think will fit in the cars?"

"Not enough."

Brianna hoisted another case. "I've got a rack on top. Do you have a tarp? We can load up the top and lash the tarp down to cover it all up."

Tracy nodded. "It's in the garage. I'll have to stop to find it."

"Do it. We'll need to hide what we have."

"All right. I'll be back as soon as I can." Tracy ran toward the door and reached for the door handle. Searing heat and pain shot her hand back. "Ow!"

"Are you all right?"

"The door handle is too hot. I can't open the door."

Brianna's eyes went wide. "That means the fire's already in the hall. We don't have much time."

Tracy stood still for a moment, the pain in her hand eclipsing all ability to think. Blisters rose on her palm in massive clumps as the skin surrounding them flared red. "I don't think I can lift any more boxes."

She turned to Brianna and the young woman rushed up to assess her hand. "We need to treat that. I've got a burn kit in my bag."

"What about the rest of the food and water?" There was still so much they could save.

"The cars must be full by now. Come on. I'll help you out the window."

Brianna moved a case of water under the window and Tracy climbed out, her hand so painful she could barely stand.

"Mom! Are you okay?" Madison rushed up to her, but Tracy waved her off. "I'm fine. I just burned my hand."

"She needs my burn kit. It's in my bag."

"I'll get it."

So many voices. Tracy couldn't think. The ground swam in front of her eyes. "We need to get the tarp. It's in… the garage."

"Mom! Mom are you okay?"

Madison's voice filtered into her ears, but it was so far away. Everything was far away: the ground, the house, the smell of smoke. Had they left home already? Were they already somewhere new?

She needed to leave a note for Walter. They couldn't rush off without telling him where to go. Tracy clutched at the hand holding her arm. "We need to tell Walter where we are. We have to go back. He needs to know…"

"Mom? You're not making any sense. Mom?"

"I think the pain's making her loopy."

When did my tongue get so big? Tracy smacked it on the roof of her mouth. "I'm not in pain. What pain?"

She wished she could see. It was so dark where they were. "Can someone turn on the light? I need to see."

"Here. Get her to take this."

Madison held something up to her lips. "Mom. You need to take these. They'll make you feel better."

A bunch of small, round things landed on her thick, fat tongue. Tracy tried to spit them out.

"No, Mom. Swallow them. Here, drink some water."

Her mouth filled with liquid and Tracy swallowed, the little round things bobbing down her throat like paper boats in the ocean. They tasted like candy. Maybe they were at the candy store that she went to once as a kid.

When an aunt she'd never met picked her up from the foster home that one time, they had taken a ride to the candy store and little Tracy had picked out all the candy she wanted.

Aunt Verna told her she was going to live somewhere new where no one would hurt her or forget to feed her or leave her at home for days on end all alone. Tracy had smiled then, and stuffed a bag so full of chocolate, little foil-wrapped pieces kept falling out.

She didn't get to eat much of it, though. The police said it was evidence.

Maybe this trip was making up for it. She smiled and tried to bring the world back into focus.

"Why is it so bright and warm?"

"The house is on fire, Mom."

"Don't be silly. We just bought it."

"I think she needs to lie down."

"Let's get her to the car. I can work on her hand there."

An arm looped through each of Tracy's and she walked along with whoever was taking her to the candy place. As they sat her down on a seat, she leaned back and closed her eyes. "I think I need a nap."

"That's all right, Mrs. Sloane. You just fall asleep now. Everything will be all right in a little bit."

"Why is she so out of it?"

"It's the pain. She delirious."

Tracy heard more voices, but couldn't make out the words. Something cool and wet coated her hand. Was she taking a bath? Not that it mattered. She was so very tired.

As she slipped into sleep, a single voice caught her ear. "Hurry up. I think someone's coming."

CHAPTER TWENTY-FOUR

WALTER

Jenkins Residence
7:00 p.m.

Walter set Drew down on the floor of his kitchen before dumping the bags off his shoulders and collapsing in a heap. Dragging a half-conscious man and two duffels up three flights of stairs while praying two bad dudes with guns didn't find you was worse than the Crucible. Worse than those two days in the box at SERE. Worse than that moment when he thought his plane was going down and he'd be dying on impact.

Drew was too damn heavy. Walter mopped up the sweat with his shirt and exhaled.

Now came the hard part. Keeping that dead weight of a co-pilot alive. He hauled himself up and began opening the kitchen cabinets. On the fifth one, he struck gold.

Leave it to an ass like Drew to be fully stocked with liquor. Walter grabbed the vodka and took a long drink before setting it on the counter. Then he moved onto drawers, pulling out a roll of duct tape, scissors, and a lighter. Now all he needed was a damn good painkiller. He found a bottle of Advil above the sink and turned to Drew.

Walter kneeled beside the man and cut away his shirt with the scissors. His flashlight sat on the table illuminating the little space in which he worked and Walter picked it up to peer at the wound.

"Through and through. Thank God." He could tape him up and hope for the best. If they found a pharmacy that still had medicine, he could pump Drew full of antibiotics. But even without them, he might make it as long as no bullet fragments remained inside.

After running the scissors through the flame of the lighter and washing down the edge of the table with the vodka, Walter cut small strips of tape and hung them off the edge. When he'd assembled about twenty, he turned to Drew.

"Sorry buddy. This is going to hurt." He grabbed the bottle of vodka and leaned Drew back. As he tilted his friend's shoulder, he poured the vodka straight into the wound.

Drew groaned and thrashed, but Walter held him tight. "What the hell are you doing?"

"Oh, hey. Look who's awake. I'm saving your life, asshole. Quick kicking."

"That hurts."

"Unfortunate side effect of getting shot."

"Am I gonna be okay?" Drew peered down at Walter's hand where he still held the vodka bottle, dribbling it into and around the wound.

"I don't know. But this will give you a chance. Looks like the bullet went clean through. Thank God that idiot shot you with an AR-15. Anything slower and you'd have a bunch of fragments stuck in there and all I'd be able to do is watch you die."

"Comforting."

"I try." Walter set the vodka down and waited for the alcohol on Drew's skin to evaporate. As soon as the skin surrounding the wound was dry, he picked up a strip of tape.

"Please tell me that's not what I think it is."

"Come on. Duct tape is one of man's greatest inventions."

"It's meant to hold things like plastic pipes together. Not my skin."

"Turns out it's got a lot of off-label uses." Walter held up the strip. "Would you rather I dig out a sewing needle and do this the old-fashioned way?"

Drew's eyes went wide.

"Didn't think so." Walter leaned closer. "All right. Brace yourself."

Drew reached out with his good hand and gripped the nearest chair leg. "Before you start, can I get some of that vodka?"

"Sure thing." Walter handed it over along with six Advil. "Take those, too."

Drew downed the little blue pills along with a hefty dose of liquor. "I'm ready."

With one hand, Walter pulled Drew's wound together. With the other, he laid the small strip of tape across. "When I'm done, the wound should stay closed, but it'll still be open to the air to breathe and ooze."

"It's going to ooze?"

"If it gets infected it will. And we want to know if that happens." He laid another strip of tape.

Drew grimaced, his face growing even paler than before.

"Hang in there, all right?"

Drew nodded and Walter laid another strip of tape. After about half an hour of careful work, Walter finished. Small strips of tape held the wound together on both sides of Drew's shoulder.

"Thanks, man."

"You're welcome. Let's not make a habit of it, okay?"

"So where's Anne?"

Walter paused. "I don't know."

Drew sat up a bit straighter. "Did you look for her?"

"Not yet. I was focused on keeping you alive."

Drew planted his good hand on the ground as if he were about to stand up.

"Whoa." Walter held up his hand. "You're not going anywhere yet. Give me five minutes. I'll take a look around."

"Thanks." Drew slumped back against the wall.

Walter stood and wiped his hands on his pants. He'd half expected when he busted in the front door that Anne would be there, safe and waiting for them. But when she didn't appear—not when Walter banged around in the kitchen or Drew cried out—he didn't have much hope.

Either she wasn't there, or…

He started in the front and worked his way to the back. Entryway, kitchen, living room, half-bath. *Empty*. Drew watched him until he ducked into the hall.

Walter cracked the first door. Guest bedroom. *Empty*. He moved on. In the hall bath, the medicine cabinet hung open. The bottles inside had been knocked about and three littered the floor.

Walter inhaled and checked his watch. Nine thirty on the fifth day without power. How long had riots been going on outside? How long had Anne been trapped inside her apartment, staring out at the chaos, losing hope that her fiancée would ever make it home?

He tensed before opening the last door. *This is it.* Walter turned the door handle and pushed it open.

The sight made him stumble.

A woman reclined on the bed, arms still against her sides, head resting on the pillow. She looked for all the world like an actress playing Snow White or Sleeping Beauty. But Anne wasn't playing.

The ashen pallor of her cheeks and the incredible stillness of her body gave her secret away. Walter walked around the bed, careful not to touch it. A note sat on the bedside table, Drew's named written in script across the front.

Walter didn't know what to do. Did he tell Drew? Did he lie and say she wasn't here? No, he couldn't do that.

Drew would need to know the truth. He would need to know that his fiancée couldn't wait for him any longer. She'd given up hope before he made it home.

"Anne!" Drew stumbled into the room, falling onto the bed as he scrabbled to touch her.

"I'm sorry, Drew."

"No!" He reached for her, the duct tape on his shoulder straining as he dragged her lifeless body into his arms. "She can't be gone." Drew kissed the top of her forehead as he cradled the woman he loved in his arms.

Walter looked out the window. From their vantage point, the city was in ruins. At least thirty fires dotted the sky, smoke billowing up white and gray against the dark night. No sound of police sirens or fire trucks.

No one was coming to douse the flames.

"She left you a note." Walter pointed at the bedside table but didn't turn around. He heard the rustle of the paper.

Drew snuffed back his emotions. "She thought I wasn't coming. She thought I must have died. That everyone had died. It was…"

He trailed off for a moment, grief and anger thickening his words.

"It was chaos here. Riots and looting. She watched a band of thugs beat a man to death for no reason. She saw a woman… oh, God."

The paper crinkled and Walter turned around. Tears streamed down Drew's cheeks and landed on his dead fiancée. "She ran out of food and water and didn't see a way out. She… she said she's sorry."

Drew pulled her dead body closer. "I'm the one who failed her and she's sorry." He rocked her back and forth, oblivious to any pain in his shoulder or Walter's patient stare.

"I'll give you a moment with her. When you're ready to talk, I'll be in the kitchen." Walter walked out of the bedroom and shut the door. Before he made it down the hall, he could hear Drew's tortured weeping.

Walter walked to the cabinet that held the liquor and pulled down the scotch. He grabbed two lowball glasses and poured them full before taking them back to the table. He sat down and sipped.

Anne's death made his mission all that more critical. He needed to find Tracy and Madison before any more time passed. The National Guard would close off downtown soon. If he didn't get out of there, he would be trapped.

The sound of the door opening caught his ear and Walter glanced up. Drew walked into the kitchen and sat down at the table. He picked up the glass of scotch waiting for him and downed it in one long, steady gulp.

He set the empty glass on the table.

"I know this is a lot to deal with, but you need to make a decision."

Drew's eyes flicked up to Walter's face. "About what?"

"Whether you're going to live or die."

"I don't follow."

"You have two options. One, you can say your goodbyes and come with me and have a shot at surviving in this new world we live in."

"Or?"

"Two, you stay here, wallowing in your grief, until the National Guard erects its perimeter and you're trapped in this hell hole with no food and no water and no way to get out."

Drew sucked in a breath.

"I can't stay here any longer, Drew. My family is still out there, waiting for me."

"Anne was my family."

"I understand that and I'm sorry. But I need to leave. I'd like your help if you can manage. But if you can't, I understand."

After a moment, Drew nodded. "All right. I'll go."

Walter exhaled. "Good. Now get some clothes, your keys, and anything else you need. We have to get your car and get out of here while we still can."

DAY SIX

CHAPTER TWENTY-FIVE

MADISON

SLOANE RESIDENCE
6:30 a.m.

THE SKY BEGAN TO GLOW ALONG THE ROOFLINE OF all the neighboring houses and Madison clutched the shotgun tighter. All that remained of her parents' house was the chimney and walls burned almost to the ground.

The refrigerator still stood, warped and useless in a city with no power grid, but their clothes, beds, furniture, and at least half of the supplies her mom had acquired were gone. Up in smoke thanks to some jerk with a vendetta.

All because Madison tied some intruder up instead of shooting him in the head. She should have killed him and strung his body up on the porch as a notice: don't mess with the Sloanes or you'll be next.

But she didn't. Instead, she'd tried to be sensible and

balance the need to protect her friends and family with the humanity that still hid inside her. There was a little bit less of it now.

"What on earth happened here?"

Madison spun around and brought the gun up to position. An older woman wearing a faded pink housecoat held up her hands. She lowered the gun. "Sorry. I'm a bit touchy."

"Madison is that you?"

She nodded. "Hi, Penny."

Penny Palmer had hosted the neighborhood meeting where Bill first showed his true colors. She wasn't like him, though. Penny had always been a good woman and kind to Madison and her mom.

She stared the smoldering ruins in disbelief. "I smelled the smoke last night, but figured someone must be out grilling. I didn't think to come check."

"The gunfire didn't tip you off?"

The woman managed a pained smile. "I turn my hearing aids off most of the time now to conserve the batteries. Is everyone okay?"

Madison sighed. "Mostly."

"Do you know what started it?"

"Looters."

Penny reached for the collar of her housecoat, pinching it shut against her neck. "Are you sure?"

"Shooting out our windows and setting the house on fire is a pretty good clue, yep." Madison was tired of this conversation. She was done with people who didn't understand. People who didn't take this new world order seriously were on the tail end of their lives. They just didn't know it yet.

Peyton wandered up from the backyard where he had set up camp after the flames died down. He smiled at Madison. "Did you sleep at all?"

"No. I wanted to make sure the fire was completely out and keep the cars safe."

He patted her on the back. "Good job. How about you go get some rest. You can use my bag. It's still out back."

"Thanks, but I'm okay. I couldn't sleep now even if I wanted to." Madison tipped her head toward the neighbors across the street. While Peyton had been talking, another two neighbors showed up. It was beginning to be a block party.

Peyton nodded. "Something I can help you ladies with?"

"Oh, we're just talking about how horrible this all is. That someone would do such a thing to the Sloanes' house." The woman speaking shook her head.

Madison snorted. "Funny. You don't seem all that troubled."

The woman's mouth fell open, but she didn't say any more.

Sometime in the middle of the night, while staring at the remains of her parents' hard work and sacrifice, Madison lost her filter. Screw being nice and polite and trying to help people.

Strangers weren't worth saving. Not now.

"Are you sure you don't want a nap?"

"Why?" Madison cast Peyton a glance. "Because I'm telling the truth for once?"

"No. Because you're acting like all those actors in those Snickers ads. The hungry ones."

Madison exhaled. "A Snickers sounds good."

"Tell me about it." Tucker walked up from the backyard, scratching his head as he came to a stop. He waved at the growing crowd. "Looks like we're the morning news."

"They haven't had the internet for almost a week. We're the most interesting thing they've seen in days." Brianna appeared and planted a kiss on Tucker's cheek.

"Blech. Stay back, gorilla breath."

"Hey, watch it." She punched Tucker in the arm. "You think if we stole some curtains and made a stage we could barter a half hour theater show for some coffee? Those assholes burned down the kitchen before I could salvage the instant."

A rush of tears welled in Madison's eyes and she fought them back. No one was going to break her down. Not anymore. Those jerks could have their little party over their senseless destruction wherever they were. She wasn't having it.

"How's your mom?"

Madison glanced at Brianna. "Sleeping still. Her hand looks pretty bad. I think she's missing some skin in places and the rest is all blistered."

"No wonder she was so out of it last night. The pain had to be incredible."

Tucker whistled through his teeth. "We're going to

need to find some antibiotics. Burns like that can get infected easily."

Madison clamped her teeth together. *Antibiotics*. Just another thing to add to the list. She turned away from the street and the gathering crowd to survey the house wreckage again. "We should poke through everything. Make sure we haven't missed anything salvageable before we leave."

"Where are we going to go?" Peyton asked the question that had lingered in the back of Madison's mind all night.

"You all are welcome at the Clifton family compound, you know that."

Madison turned to Brianna. "I can't ask your family to take us in. That's a lot of extra mouths to feed."

"I didn't say you won't work for your supper. It takes a lot of labor to live off the grid."

Madison reached out and wrapped Brianna up in a hug. "Thanks for the offer."

Brianna pushed her away. "You're welcome. But no hugging with the paparazzi about."

With a laugh, Madison glanced back at the crowd. "Ugh. When did he get here?"

Brianna turned. "Who?"

"Bill Donovan. You know, the guy who threatened to kill us? The one who supposedly did all of this. Of all people to rubberneck."

Peyton grumbled. "Want me to take him out? I bet that baseball bat survived. One good swing is all it would take."

"No one is taking anyone out." Madison said it as

much to remind herself as to ward off any heroics from Peyton. Killing Bill might give her an immediate rush of satisfaction, but did she want his blood on her hands?

Most likely scenario, he'd die soon anyway.

She glanced at all the people standing around. So would most of them. Madison shook her head. "Let's just tell them all to leave and then we can wake up my mom and pack up."

Tucker walked toward the crowd. "There's nothing to see, so if everyone could respect our privacy and leave, we would appreciate it."

Brianna snorted. "He's being too nice."

"These people haven't done anything to us." Peyton shrugged. "He's just being decent."

"That one has." Brianna crossed her arms, looking every bit the smug twenty-year-old a man like Bill Donovan couldn't stand.

His voice rang out over the crowd. "Do you all need any assistance? A place to stay? I'm sure we could arrange something."

"Right. And I'm Polly-f'ing-anna."

"Stop it." Madison hissed at Brianna. "He's offering an olive branch."

"No; he's scouting for information. He wants to know if we're still a threat."

Madison called out. "Thanks, but we're okay. We'll be packing up and leaving today."

Bill's gaze cut to the two cars parked on the street. "Those cars look pretty full. Are you sure you all can fit?"

"Here we go." Brianna toyed with a lock of her hair, a smile practically popping off her face.

"We'll be fine. Thanks." Madison turned away, signaling the end of the conversation, but Bill didn't give up.

"If you all have too much stuff, I'm sure there are people in the neighborhood who could use it."

Madison froze, one foot in the air. She set it down and spun around. "Excuse me?"

"You seem to have plenty. You could stop being so greedy and spread the wealth."

Oh hells, no. Madison cracked her knuckles and hoisted the shotgun into plain sight before marching up to the edge of her parents' property. "Let me get this straight."

As soon as she began to talk, the crowd of neighbors parted like the Red Sea and Bill stood exposed and alone. His white hair stood out in contrast to the black of his shirt and his personality. Madison wished more than anything that she could shoot him where he stood.

She made a show of raising the shotgun. The sound of Brianna racking her pump action brought a smile to Madison's face. It wasn't friendly. "My parents' house burns down last night, a fire set by people attempting to break in, and you have the audacity to stand there and ask us to give you something?"

Bill shifted in his stance. "It only seems fair."

"Fair? You want to talk about fairness?" She eased forward, anger rising despite her earlier attempts to talk herself down. "While you all were out there doing goodness knows what, my mother was risking her life to get the supplies we had. She was attacked and could have been killed. Thanks to the fire, she's got massive burns on her hand that need medical attention."

Madison paused to point at her friends. "The four of us risked our lives to bring what we did, driving here from Davis, almost getting run off the causeway and shot at in a convenience store."

"What's your point?"

"My point is that you're a coward. We risk everything so that we have food and water and emergency supplies and you stand there in your polo shirt and driving moccasins asking for us to share. Show me how far you're willing to go to survive and then we can talk."

"You don't know anything about me."

Madison stood her ground, heart thundering in her chest. "You're right. I don't. How about you fill me in? Were you the one who tried to break in last night? Were you the one who set the fire?" She lowered her head to line up the sight on barrel with the buttons on Bill's polo shirt. "One of our friends died in the fight. Did you murder her?"

A gasp went up in the crowd around Bill, rushed questions and outrage flying around like a sudden swarm of locusts.

"Is that true?"

"Did someone die?"

"Who was it?"

"Bill, you didn't…"

Bill's mouth opened in outrage, but he shut it just as

fast. "I don't have to listen to this. You have no right to accuse me of anything."

Madison's finger trigger itched. She wanted to shoot him so badly. Make him suffer for what he did to Wanda. Memories of her lifeless body and Tucker's blood-soaked hands filled Madison's mind. Her vision blurred. "Not good enough. I need an answer. Did you do it? Did you kill her?"

"Madison, maybe you should—"

She swung the shotgun around and pointed it at Tucker. "He shouldn't get away with it."

"But if you kill him, you won't be any better than him. Wanda's gone. I know. Her life slipped through my fingers. Killing Bill won't bring her back."

"It would feel damn good, though."

Tucker nodded. "For now. But what about tomorrow? Or the day after? You'll have to live with that guilt forever."

Madison twisted back around, the barrel of the shotgun parading over the faces in the crowd. A little girl of no more than five stood a few feet from Bill, her arms wrapped around her mother's thigh. Madison paused, concern drawing her brows together.

So many innocent people. None of them had any clue as to how the world was changing. They would learn soon enough. Madison didn't need to be the one to bring it about. She focused on the little girl, her brown hair the same shade as Madison's own.

She couldn't kill a man in front of a child. No matter how much he deserved it. With a jagged exhale, she lowered the shotgun and focused on Bill. "This conversation is over."

As she stepped back, Madison took a moment to look over all the faces in the crowd. "If any one of you so much as steps a foot onto Sloane property or touches one of our cars, so help me God, I'll drop you where you stand. Is that clear?"

The crowd murmured, heads averted and bent. The little girl ducked behind her mother, a flash of the pale yellow dress she wore the only evidence she even existed. In moments, the crowd dispersed, people walking back to their homes in groups of two and three.

Tucker appeared by her side. "Thanks, Madison."

"Don't thank me yet. If that man so much as looks our way, I declare it just cause."

Brianna walked up and clapped Madison on the shoulder. "Good job reigning it in, babe. I wouldn't have been so neighborly."

Madison exhaled and turned toward the cars. It had taken all her strength not to shoot. She hoped she wouldn't regret it. "Come on. We need to check on my mom. She should be awake by now."

CHAPTER TWENTY-SIX

WALTER

Downtown Sacramento
6:00 a.m.

"We're never gonna get out of here."

Walter cast Drew an irritated glance. "Not with that attitude, we're not."

"Come on. It took us three hours to get out of the parking deck." Drew eased back in the passenger seat, wincing as he bumped his wounded shoulder.

Walter grunted. "You try moving a burned-out car all by yourself. It's not as easy as it looks."

From the attitude Drew was giving him, Walter half-wished he'd just let the man die. So far he had been zero help. He knew the man had a bullet wound and he had just lost his soon-to-be wife, but still. He could have put in a bit more effort.

Thanks to his complete lack of preparedness at his

condo, they weren't even able to scrounge up any food. His fiancée had been right—they had nothing. The extra clothes, lighters, and liquor would come in handy, but what Walter could really use was a Gatorade and a Power Bar.

He exhaled and eased the car down another alley. The little side streets proved to be less congested than the main streets: fewer rioters out looking to wreak havoc or cars stuck in the middle of the road.

So far the alley ahead appeared clear. If they could only make it to the highway, they had a chance to get out of downtown. As Walter eased the little Volkswagen between the buildings, he flicked his eyes up to the rear view.

A small light wavered behind him, roving over the alley and lingering on the back of their car. *Shit.* He pushed the accelerator down, increasing the speed from a slow crawl of fifteen to forty.

Drew shifted in his seat. "What are you doing?"

"Someone's behind us." Walter kept glancing at the rear view while navigating around the trash cans and dumpsters and intermittent debris in the alley as best he could. One fender hit a trash can and sent it flying into the air.

It slammed to the ground with a bang and a clatter.

"Hey! Watch it! My car's only a year old."

Walter snorted. "I don't think you need to worry about resale value."

"You have a point." Drew turned to stare out the window. After a moment, he eased closer to the window. "Hey… Walter?"

"Yeah?"

"I think we've got another problem."

"What?"

Drew leaned closer to the glass, glancing behind him and then out to the side again. "There's a motorcycle on our tail. No lights."

Walter squinted into the just-before-dawn light. "I don't see anything."

"It's keeping to the shadows. I saw it in a reflection in a window."

"Can you tell what it's doing?"

Drew struggled to turn in the seat and keep his shoulder immobilized. "No. I only caught a glimpse once or twice. Single driver. Helmet covering the entire face. I can't tell if he's armed."

Walter frowned. The light in the rear view still tracked them, bouncing up and down as if it were traveling on the same road. "I think they're together. The light behind us must be a motorcycle as well." He checked his watch. "It'll be light enough to see in a few minutes. Hopefully they hold back until then."

"If they don't?"

"Ever been in a high-speed chase?"

"No. Have you?"

"Only in the air." Walter glanced at Drew's torso. "Buckle up. This could get dangerous."

Drew laughed. "Like it isn't already." He reached for the seatbelt and pulled it over his chest, easing it under his arm and wounded shoulder before buckling. "Okay. I'm ready."

Walter hit the gas. "Good. Because we're going to lose these two right now."

The car lurched as it picked up speed and Walter gripped the steering wheel with both hands, holding it steady at ten and two. Driving wasn't that different than flying, if he thought about it. He couldn't do the same evasive maneuvers since the car couldn't exactly leave the horizontal plane, but he wasn't scared to push the car to its limits.

Multi-ton machines were built to handle a lot more than most people put them through. He glanced at Drew. Some people, in particular.

Walter punched the gas as the car came to a main road, flying over the curb and bottoming out in the middle of the street. Drew grunted next to him and reached for the handle above the window.

"You all right?"

"Fine."

"Are they still coming?"

Drew turned around. "Yes, and you're right. There's two of them. One looks like a Harley or something similar, lots of chrome and pipes. The other is a crotch rocket, built for speed."

Walter cursed. "We could outmaneuver and outrun the Harley, but we'll never escape the racer." He glanced at the time: 6:40. "It's sunrise. They won't be able to hide in the shadows anymore."

He barreled down the next alley, swerving around a dumpster tipped on its side before hitting another street. They bounced over the curb, the tail pipes scraping as he turned the wheel. "Let's see how they do out in the open."

The car fishtailed as he whipped it onto the road and he hit some burned-out hunk of metal before he got it under control. The riot had died out some time in the morning hours, at least in this part of downtown. Not a soul was on the road except them and the two motorcycles.

The Harley behind them growled as it sped up. Walter glanced in the rear view. "I don't see any weapons."

"Then what's the point?"

"I'm guessing they hope we crash."

The street racer screeched and bucked before accelerating toward them. Walter slowed.

"What are you doing?"

"Seeing what they're after."

Drew braced himself in the seat, slinking down to hide most of his body beneath the window.

The bike came up even with the driver's side, the red and black body dented and scraped. Walter couldn't make out any features of the driver. The black visor of the helmet blocked his view.

"Walter!"

"What?" Walter snapped his gaze away.

"The Harley has a gun!"

Walter glanced up at the rear view. *Crap*. While he'd been distracted by the street bike, the other driver had pulled out a shotgun and aimed it at the car. With a clear road behind them, the Harley driver had a clear shot.

Walter squeezed the steering wheel. "I'd duck, if I were you."

Drew crouched down in the seat, clutching the console like it would somehow protect him.

The first shot went wide, hitting the passenger-side mirror and splintering it in a million pieces. Drew jumped. "They're shooting at us!"

"Yes, they are." Walter flicked his gaze back and forth between the motorcycle next to him, the one behind them, and the road in front. It was too much. He clipped a tipped-over fridge and the car lurched to the left, coming within a foot of the motorcycle.

The driver swerved and kept the bike upright, but it gave Walter an idea. A tipped car sat on its side about two blocks ahead, debris and wreckage strewn all around it. "How far are we from the highway?"

Drew rose up enough to catch the street sign as they passed. "Less than a mile."

"Hold on." Walter headed straight for the wrecked car and punched the accelerator.

"What are you doing?"

"Increasing our odds." He glanced at the street bike next to him. *Good luck staying on, buddy.* As the little Jetta picked up speed, Walter angled away from the debris as if he were trying to avoid it. The motorcycle stayed by his side as the driver leaned over, concentrating on keeping up.

That's it. Stay with me. One block passed in a blur. The car sat a hundred yards away. Seventy-five. Fifty. Walter gripped the steering wheel. He'd need to time it just right. Twenty-five.

He darted around the worst of the large debris—a fender or side wall—and resumed course. Fifteen yards. Ten.

Walter sucked in a breath and swerved, aiming the driver's side of the Jetta right for the tipped-over car. The driver of the street racer rose up and tried to turn, but it was too late.

"You're gonna hit it!" Drew screamed as Walter kept the wheel steady. "We're gonna—"

At the last second, Walter cranked the wheel, clipping the front bumper of the wreck, but not hitting it full-on. The motorcycle rider wasn't so lucky. As he tried to dodge the car by leaning far to the left, his tires lost their grip on the road.

The motorcycle skidded along the pavement, driver still clutching the handlebars, body twisted for the turn. Walter looked away at impact. He didn't need to watch to know the man would never survive.

The wrecked car wobbled in the rear view, tilting back and forth until it crashed onto the ground. The Harley slowed, stopping at the site of the crash.

Drew eased up from his crouch near the floorboards and looked out the rear window. "Holy shit, you did it!"

Walter exhaled. It wasn't exactly like flying a plane, but it was as close as he'd get for a good long while. As his heart rate slowed, he saw the on-ramp to the freeway ahead. An Army vehicle sat on the inbound ramp, and from their distance, Walter could barely make out men milling about.

The defensive perimeter.

He glanced at Drew. "You up for one more race?"

Drew groaned. "Do I have a choice?"

"Nope." Walter punched the gas again, not bothering to look at how much fuel his evasive maneuvers cost. They were getting out of downtown in a vehicle, no matter what.

A group of guardsmen dragged a chain-link fence into position on the highway ramp, tying it into a section of fence just beyond. The gap was closing. Walter increased their speed.

He closed the distance between them and the soldiers in seconds. A group of them stopped at his approach, some reaching for their weapons, others merely staring, mouths open. He rolled down the window and stuck out his hand in a wave as they blew past the crowd.

No one fired. Walter darted under the overpass and onto the frontage road running alongside the opposite side of the highway. They were out of downtown. They were free.

He slowed the vehicle to a safe speed. With any luck, he'd be hugging his wife and daughter soon.

CHAPTER TWENTY-SEVEN

TRACY

Sloane Residence
    7:30 a.m.

"Just a little while longer, mamma. I'm so tired." Tracy rolled over and tried to tug the covers up on her little twin bed.

"Mom, it's me, Madison. You're dreaming. You need to wake up."

Tracy frowned in her sleep. "Go away. I want to sleep."

"No. Please wake up."

After a minute or two of constant shaking and talking at her, Tracy finally blinked an eye open. "Madison? What's going on?"

"You were asleep."

Tracy sat up, but the pounding in her head and hand made her wince and falter.

Madison rushed in to keep her from falling back over. "Easy. I've got you."

"My head is killing me."

"What about your hand?"

Tracy squinted and tried to focus on her burn, but the pain her head made it difficult. "It hurts, too."

Madison reached for Tracy's injured hand and she held it out. Her daughter examined it. "You need antibiotics and some painkillers."

"Do we have any?"

"No. We lost it all in the fire."

Tracy groaned. She couldn't help the kids in this state.

"Excuse me, Madison?"

Tracy tried to stand up, but her daughter touched her shoulder to tell her no. "Who is that?"

"Penny from across the street. Hold on."

Madison stepped away and Tracy tried to get it together. Her daughter and friends needed her coherent and functional, not discombobulated and worthless. She scooted forward on the seat and a wave of nausea gripped her.

Tracy leaned back until it subsided, forced to do nothing but keep still.

A few minutes later, Madison returned. She handed her an open bottle of water and Tracy took a sip.

"What did Penny want?"

Madison smiled. "To help, actually. She brought you some Advil and antibiotics. She said they're expired, but they might still work." Madison held up the little brown bottle. "Said they gave her hives so she quit taking them after only two days."

Tracy held out her good hand and Madison put two pills in her palm. "Better than nothing."

After Tracy swallowed the pain pills and the antibiotics, she eased back onto the seat. "Give me a few minutes, okay?"

Madison nodded. "Sure thing. We're going to check the house for anything salvageable. Just yell if you need anything."

Tracy nodded and closed her eyes. Everything had gone so terribly wrong. After all she had been through, getting supplies, picking up Wanda, stealing the little Nissan. And someone had to ruin it.

She pried an eye open and glanced at the still-smoldering remains of her house. They would have to leave.

The thought sent a new wave of nausea up her throat and Tracy worked to hold it down. Walter was out there somewhere. She could feel it in her heart and bones. Her husband was out there in the chaos, trying to get home.

But when he got there, they would be gone. He would show up to an empty, burned-out house, and think the worst. If only there were some way they could stay. If only the house hadn't burned all the way to the ground or they hadn't captured that man to begin with or…

Tracy shook her head. She could run through a million different what-ifs but it wouldn't change the facts. They had to move on.

She leaned back and closed her eyes. All she needed was a few minutes more rest.

* * *

2:00 P.M.

TRACY BLINKED HER EYES OPEN. SHE WAS STILL IN THE same place as that morning, sitting in the passenger side of the Nissan, burned hand lying palm-up in her lap. She glanced at her watch. Two in the afternoon? *Did I sleep all day?*

She pushed the door open and swung her legs out of the car.

"Mom! Hold on! Don't try to stand up."

Tracy scoffed as her daughter ran over. "Don't be silly. I'm fine." She pushed herself up to stand as Madison stuttered to a stop in front of her.

"Are you feeling better?"

Tracy nodded. "Whatever Penny gave me seems to be working."

Her daughter exhaled in relief. "Thank goodness. I didn't know what we were going to do if you didn't get better."

"Where is everyone?"

"Tucker is charging his solar panels. He spent the morning hooking up all his computer equipment and trying to find a trace of the internet or a radio station or anything out there somewhere."

"Any luck?"

"Nope."

Tracy nodded. It was what she had come to accept. There wasn't a reset button for this kind of disaster. "How about Brianna and Peyton?"

"Brianna gathered all the guns and ammo and set about organizing it all. Now we know what we have and she fashioned little ammo sacks out of one of her T-shirts so we can sync up the right gun with the right ammunition."

"Good."

"Peyton and I are searching the house. We found some cans in the master that survived and a few things in the garage. That's about it."

Tracy paused. She didn't know how to bring up the obvious. "What about Wanda?"

Her daughter glanced at the ground. "We left my bedroom alone. I couldn't—" The tremor in Madison's voice twisted Tracy's insides. Wanda hadn't been with them long, but she had become more than a boss, she had become a friend. Tracy held up her hand. "It's okay. As soon as you are ready, we should head out."

Madison's head popped up, her eyes wide and wet with unshed tears. "What do you mean?"

Tracy glanced at the remains of her home. "We can't stay here. Whoever set the fire might be coming back to finish the job. And we need shelter. Our cars aren't big enough to hold our supplies and us forever."

Her daughter blinked quickly. "I'm sorry, Mom. It's all my fault. If I hadn't—"

"Shush. It is not. You didn't set the fire. You didn't

break into our house. What's done is done. There's no use dwelling on it. All we can do is move forward."

"What about Dad?"

Tracy hesitated. "I'm going to talk to Penny and see if she'll keep an eye out. If your father does show up, she can at least point him in the right direction."

Her daughter nodded and turned to go, but Tracy stopped her. "Madison?"

"Yeah?" As she turned back around, Tracy smiled. Her daughter might be nineteen, but she still looked at her with the big, eager eyes of a child.

"Your father will find us. I know it."

Madison nodded, but didn't say anything else before turning away. Tracy knew her daughter's hope was fading. But Tracy wasn't giving up. Walter would find them eventually.

She smoothed the hair off her face with her good hand and examined the burn for the first time with a level head. Based on the pain she experienced and the blistering without charring, it appeared to only be second-degree.

Not that a second-degree burn couldn't kill her if it got infected, but it could be worse. A third-degree burn would have meant she burned through all the layers of her skin and would have nerve damage and charring. She wouldn't feel a thing because there wouldn't be anything left.

Never in her life was Tracy more thankful for excruciating pain. If she could keep the wound clean, it would heal in a few weeks. She just needed to pay attention.

After drinking an entire bottle of water, Tracy found a scrap of paper and scribbled a note on it and shoved it in her pocket. Then she managed to pick up the case of water, balance it on her hip, and make her way across the street.

Penny had always been a good friend. She remembered the cookies she brought over the very first day Tracy and Walter moved in. Butterscotch chocolate chip.

She didn't even have to knock, Penny opened the door with a smile. "Hi, Tracy."

"Hi, Penny. I wanted to thank you for the medicine."

"Is it helping?"

"Yes. I want you to have this in return." She twisted her hip and stuck out the case. "I'm afraid I can't hand it to you, but you can take it."

The wrinkles around Penny's eyes deepened. "I don't want to take your water. You have so many more mouths to look after."

"Please take it. It's the least I can offer."

After a moment, Penny reached out and took the case with a smile. "Thank you."

"You're welcome."

After chatting for a few minutes, Tracy glanced back at the burned-out house. "We're leaving in a few hours and I'm wondering if you can do me a favor."

"Anything."

"If you see Walter," Tracy paused, trying to keep her voice even, "can you tell him we're headed north to Truckee? I've written the address down." She held out the scrap of paper. "Tell him we're sticking to the side roads."

Penny took the piece of paper and nodded. "I'll watch for him."

"Thank you."

Tracy said her goodbyes and made her way back across the street. There was still one more thing she needed to do before they left.

As she kneeled outside of what remained of Madison's bedroom, each one of the kids made their way over. She didn't need to say a word; they knew. She spent a few minutes staring at the ashes, but Wanda's bones couldn't be seen. She didn't know if the fire burned so hot there that they were gone, or if other debris covered them up. They didn't have time to look.

Madison reached out and squeezed her good hand and Tracy fought back tears.

"Wanda was a good woman. She might not have been prepared for this new world, but she gave all that she had when asked. Thanks to her, we were able to defend ourselves, stock up on our supplies, and even take a shower."

Everyone gathered around smiled and laughed through the pain of loss.

"Although she's no longer with us, she won't be forgotten." Tracy said a silent prayer and reached out to touch the charred edge of the wall. Madison and the others did the same.

"To Wanda and her sacrifice."

After a moment, Tracy stood. "All right everyone.

Let's pack up and move out while there's still some daylight left."

Brianna, Tucker, and Peyton all headed toward the Wrangler. Madison stayed behind with Tracy.

"Do you really think Dad will find us?"

Tracy nodded. "I do. No matter where we go, he'll be looking. He's a survivor, honey, just like us."

Madison nodded. "Okay." As they reached the Nissan, Madison turned around, peering into the wreckage.

"What is it?"

"I was hoping to spot Fireball, but I guess he didn't make it out in time."

Tracy paused. She'd forgotten all about the little cat. She snuffed back a fresh wave of tears. "Maybe it's for the best. I don't know how we would have fed him, anyway."

Madison wiped at her eyes. "You're probably right. But I could sure use a furry little hug right now."

Tracy reached out and squeezed her daughter's arm. "So could I. Come on, let's go."

They both slid into the car, Madison behind the wheel. The back seat was stuffed to the ceiling with what they had managed to salvage. It was a paltry amount compared to what they had before, but at least it was something.

Brianna started the Jeep in front of them and Madison stuck her thumb up out the window. They moved off the curb and onto the road, one after the other. Tracy took one last look out the window, watching until the remains of her house disappeared from view.

CHAPTER TWENTY-EIGHT

MADISON

North of Sacramento, CA
    4:00 p.m.

Trying to get out of Sacramento was like threading a camel through the eye of a needle. Every road out of town was either blocked with a multi-car accident or an endless stream of vehicles abandoned with no signs of drivers anywhere.

It had been fine on little neighborhood streets, but the major roads were virtually impassable. Brianna's Jeep could off-road around the worst of it, but the little Nissan hugged the ground and couldn't even jump the curb. Every time Brianna went around something, Madison would honk and wave and Brianna would have to backtrack. Frustration ran high in both vehicles.

After passing another clump of empty cars, Madison shook her head in amazement. "Where is everyone?"

Her mom shrugged. "Who knows? My guess is most people ran out of gas and took off on foot."

Madison reached for the radio and clicked it on. She spun the dial, searching for anything other than endless static. After a few minutes of failure, she turned it off. "Do you think we'll ever come back from this?"

"The loss of power?"

She nodded. "Think about all the things we took for granted. Food, water, heat and air." She pointed at the radio. "Music and movies and the internet. Never in a million years would I have thought the world could be as quiet as it is now."

Her mom managed a wistful smile. "I miss the radio, too. All the songs we used to sing." She turned in the passenger seat. "Do you remember when you were little and we would sing every Paul Simon song that came on?"

"I loved Paul Simon."

"The whole reason we got the CD player for the Suburban was so you could listen to his greatest hits while riding back there in your car seat. I couldn't see you—the car was so big and your seat faced the back—but I could hear your happy little voice belt out every word to Diamonds on the Soles of Her Shoes."

Madison choked back a sob. So many memories. So many things she took for granted. "Do you think it's the whole country? If we drove to Seattle or Alaska, would it be better there?"

"I don't know. It depends on the size of the EMP, I suppose."

"Brianna said if it had been a nuclear attack, parts

of the US would still have power, like Florida and maybe even Washington State."

"But this wasn't a nuclear attack. It was the sun. Truth is, we might never know unless we drive there."

Madison nodded. They had so many decisions to make, starting with where to go next. "Do you really think Brianna's family will let us stay with them?"

Her mom thought it over. "Maybe. But that depends on if her family even made it to the cabin. They could be on the road just like we are, or worse. Once we get there, we can reassess and decide what to do. Until then, we need to focus on the drive."

The car beeped and Madison glanced down. The dash flashed with a red little shape that looked like an electrical plug. "Mom?"

"Yes, dear."

"We might have a problem." Madison glanced up. About fifty yards ahead, the Jeep eased around a car blocking half of the right lane and kept going. The Leaf shuddered, the beeping from the dash growing louder and more insistent.

"I think the battery is dying."

"What?" Her mom sat up in the passenger seat. "I thought this was one of those hybrids you could drive forever and never need to stop at the gas station."

Madison hesitated. "Does it even take gas?"

"What kind of car doesn't take gas? It has to." Her mom reached for the glove box and popped it open. "Let me check the owner's manual." She fished around the dark with a frown. "Where is it?"

While her mom rooted through the glove

compartment, Madison stared at the little flashing light. The car began to shake. She pressed down on the accelerator, but the car didn't speed up. If anything, it slowed even more.

At last, her mom pulled out a business card. "For more information, including a compete owner's manual, please look us up online." She groaned. "You've got to be kidding me."

Madison pumped the gas pedal as the Leaf coasted to a stop. The battery symbol on the dash glowed solid red for a moment before blinking out. The whole car shut off.

Her mom pushed open the passenger-side door. "There has to be a gas tank. We'll just find a car, siphon it, and be back on the road in no time." She climbed out and began looking at the rear of the vehicle. "Madison? Is there a gas tank up front? I'm not seeing a place to put the hose."

Madison climbed out and glanced around. "I don't think there is a gas tank, mom."

"Nonsense." Her mom walked around the car inspecting every curve and indent before stopping back where she started. "I never."

Madison glanced up. The bright yellow of Brianna's Jeep was nowhere to be found. *Oh, no. I forgot to honk.* Madison rushed back inside the car and slammed her hand down on the horn. It stayed silent.

She hit it again. *Come on.* With the battery dead, not even the horn worked. If Brianna made it too far down the road before she noticed they were gone, she might lose track of the way back. *We could be stranded.*

"Brianna's gone."

"What?" Her mom glanced up, the space between her brows knitting together. "As soon as she notices we aren't behind her, she'll come back."

"What if she doesn't?"

Her mom glanced at the back of the Leaf loaded down with supplies. "We can stay here for the night and pack out in the morning."

"What about all the stuff?"

Her mom shrugged. "We'll have to leave it behind."

Something inside Madison snapped. *That's it!*

She kicked the side of the car as hard as she could, putting a boot-sized dent in the fender. She kicked it again and added another. "I'm so sick of this! I'm dirty and smelly, our house just burned down, my dad could be anywhere from here to Hong Kong, and now we can't even go anywhere."

Her mom didn't say a word.

"I want everything back. Movies and arcades and grocery stores and cheesy pop songs and cars... that... take... gas!" Madison accented each of her last few words with another kick to the fender. By the time she finished the poor thing looked like a giant pockmarked golf ball.

She exhaled and palmed her hips. "What?"

"Are you done?"

"Yes." She crossed her arms across her chest.

"You can scream if you want to. I know I've done it

a time or two."

Madison let her arms drop. "You've gotten so frustrated you yelled?"

"At the top of my lungs. Even threw in some choice obscenities, too." Her mom smiled. "It's okay to be frustrated. It's just never okay to give up."

The rumbling of an engine caught Madison's ear and she turned her head. The bright yellow of a familiar Jeep's front grille made her smile. "They came back!"

"Of course they did. Now help me push this car over into the parking lot. We can stop here for the night."

Madison waved at Brianna before going to the back of the Leaf and giving it a push. Her mom steered it over to the side and into the lot of what used to be a restaurant. The windows to the place had been smashed and the inside burned. Now it was an empty shell just like their former house.

Brianna parked alongside and all three college students got out. "What happened?"

"Battery's dead."

Brianna glanced around. "It takes gas, too, right? We can just siphon some and—"

Madison held up her hand. "No gas. Turns out it's electric only."

Her roommate's mouth fell open. "Of all the cars to steal, you all get an electric one? You do know the power's out, right?"

Madison's mom laughed. "It was the best I could do at the time. Believe me, I'd much rather have my Suburban."

Peyton spoke up. "We have way too much stuff to fit into the Jeep. And if we're all going to be riding in it, we'll have to take out even more. What are we going to do?"

Madison glanced at her mom. "My mom wants to stay here for the night and figure out a plan in the morning."

Tucker glanced at his watch. "Not a bad idea. It'll be getting dark in an hour or so."

Peyton nodded. "I don't think we should drive at night."

Brianna crossed her arms. "Last time we tried sleeping in our car, we almost got arrested."

"And shot," Tucker added. "Don't forget shot."

"We can take turns as a lookout. One person every two hours. That way we all get some much-needed sleep and we stay secure."

Madison nodded. "It's a good idea. I'm exhausted. You all must be too." At this point, all of them had been awake for way, way too long.

At last, Brianna dropped her hands. "Fine. I could use some sleep. But Peyton sleeps in the Leaf. I can't listen to him snore."

"I don't snore!"

"Do too!"

"Do not!"

Madison shook her head and turned toward the car. She could make Peyton some room.

Her mom spoke over the bickering. "If you all will stop arguing long enough to get us something to eat, I'll take the first shift tonight."

CHAPTER TWENTY-NINE

WALTER

<small>SLOANE RESIDENCE</small>
8:30 p.m.

WALTER SLOWED THE CAR, DISBELIEF EASING HIS FOOT off the accelerator. It couldn't be. He pulled up in front of the charred remains of a house, frowning as he glanced at the surrounding untouched homes.

"Whoa. Looks like whoever lived there got a bit too happy with the gas grill, maybe."

"That's my house."

"What?"

"You heard me." Walter turned off the car and got out, walking in slow-motion around the back. He stopped at the edge of the singed lawn.

My house.

He inhaled a shaky breath, exhaling through his mouth. All that remained of the little bungalow he and

Tracy had purchased with the proceeds from the sale of their big house out in the suburbs was a half-melted fridge and a few charred walls.

My house is gone.

Walter lifted his foot, about to step onto the grass, but he hesitated, the sole of his shoe hovering an inch above the blackened blades. Had his wife and daughter died in the fire? Were their bones lying in a charcoal heap not thirty feet in front of him?

It smelled fresh, like a campfire the morning after. Had this happened only yesterday?

If he hadn't gotten on that damn airplane... If he hadn't let his sense of duty to the job and the passengers sway him from his instincts...

Walter slid to his knees and the burnt lawn crunched beneath his jeans. *If I hadn't saved Drew...*

As the door to the Jetta opened, Walter jumped up, half-running, half-staggering into the ashes. He needed to see it. Touch it. Smell it.

To confirm with his own eyes and fingers and lips and nose that he let his family down. That he failed. He rushed into what used to be the kitchen. The fire consumed everything it touched. No kitchen table, no counters, no framed portrait of his daughter at her high school graduation.

Everything he loved. *Gone.* Walter tore into what used to be the living room and turned around in a circle. A shell of the couch still remained, the springs from the sleeper sofa inside still coiled in their cage.

Down the hall, the bathtub still sat in its familiar

position, enamel melted away to expose the iron underneath. He felt like that tub. Burned and raw. Burnt to the bone.

Walter paused outside what used to be the master. He couldn't go in. He couldn't confirm what he already knew.

"Walter!"

He turned around.

"Walter, is that you?"

A flashlight beam came bounding across the street, illuminating a pair of slipper-clad feet. He walked toward the light.

"Penny?"

"Oh, it is you! Thank goodness. Tracy asked me to look out for you and I was just about to go to bed. If you'd arrived any later, I'd have missed you."

He blinked. "Tracy? She's alive?"

"Oh, heavens, yes." She paused and looked past him at what was left of his house. "You didn't think—oh, no, Tracy and the kids are fine."

"The kids?"

"Mm-hmm, all those nice college friends of your daughter's. That one boy who looks like a football player, wow, he sure can lift some heavy things."

Walter had no idea if Penny had lost her mind or what, but he'd cling to the hope she offered. "My daughter was here? Madison was here?"

"Oh, yes. With three of her friends." Penny tucked a strand of hair up into the sleeping cap on her head. "I'm not so sure about the teeny blonde; she's a bit of a spitfire. But the other boy seems nice."

Walter exhaled. His wife and daughter were alive. He didn't care whether they had taken in the entire UC Davis Agriculture Department as long as they were still breathing.

"Do you know where they went?"

"Tracy said something about Truckee. She's driving a little foreign car and the blonde girl is in a bright yellow Jeep. It looks like a mini school bus." Penny dug one hand in her pocket and fished out a crumpled up piece of paper. She held it out to Walter. "Here. Tracy told me to give you this."

Walter took the piece of paper and opened it.

Hi, Babe.

If you're reading this, then I'm the happiest woman in the whole world. As you can see, we had to move out. A bit of a problem with the roof and whatnot. We are headed up to a cabin in Truckee. We'll be taking back roads.

Come find us.

Love you,

Tracy

Walter choked back a sob. She was alive. It didn't matter if he had to spend the rest of his life tracking her down. He would.

Walter tucked the precious piece of paper in his pocket and smiled. "Thank you, Penny. I don't know what I'd have done without you." He reached out and wrapped the tiny woman up in a hug, almost picking her up off the ground in his thanks.

"Oooh. That's okay." She patted him on the arm and Walter let her go. "Just go find your family. I know they miss you."

"I miss them, too. Thank you, again. If there's anything I can do…"

"No. Just go. I'll be fine."

Walter smiled and thanked Penny once more before rushing back to the car. He slid into the driver's seat and turned to Drew.

He took one look at the man and froze. "What the hell is that?"

Drew glanced down at the orange fur ball snuggled up on his lap. "It's a cat."

"What's it doing in our car?"

Drew raised an eyebrow. "First, it's my car. Second, he's sleeping. I opened the door to get some air while you were… busy… and he hopped right in. Didn't seem right to kick him out."

Walter exhaled. His daughter did love pets. "All right. He can stay. But he stays on your side of the car."

"Fine by me." Drew glanced out the window at the house. "I don't know how to ask, but… your family?"

"Are alive. They left this afternoon for Truckee."

Drew nodded and looked away.

Walter frowned. He couldn't imagine what Drew must be going through after losing his fiancée, but from the few minutes of panic and despair he'd just suffered through, it had to be almost unbearable. "I'm sorry about Anne, Drew. I know this must be hard."

He nodded. "It is. But you were right. I need to keep going. She wouldn't have wanted me to quit."

"So you're fine with going to find them?"

Drew shrugged. "Where else am I going to go?"

Walter turned the car back on and smiled. "All right. Road trip it is. Still buckled?"

"With you driving? You better believe it."

Walter pulled out from the curb. "Then let's go find my family."

DAY SEVEN

CHAPTER THIRTY

MADISON

Somewhere North of Sacramento, CA
5:00 a.m.

Madison couldn't sleep even if she wanted to. All she could think about was the fire. Every time she closed her eyes, flames leapt across the blackness and her eyelids popped back open.

She walked around the cars, pacing along the faded parking spot lines. The sun would be up soon, but until then, her mom and friends needed to sleep.

As she leaned against the fender of the dead electric car, she started a running tally in her head of all the things she used to take for granted and would never get to do again. No more radio or television. No more late nights cramming for a test with her friends over cold pizza and soda. No more pizza, period.

First dates and homecoming games. School plays

and art exhibits. Ice cream. So many more fun things. But then there were the basics. Running water and flushing toilets. Trash pickup. Antibiotics.

All of that was simple. The rest boggled her mind. The technology the country relied on every single day. The stock exchange. The modern banking system. Email and text messages and everything else they did with the power of electricity.

The economy would never come back from this.

A week without power and even the most stalwart supporters of the government must be doubting their sanity. No FEMA trucks rolled by. No military personnel were out patrolling the streets or delivering cases of water and MREs.

This wasn't like a hurricane or an earthquake or a flash flood. The worst natural disaster their county had faced in recent years didn't wipe out the entire power grid for thousands of miles. There was always someone, somewhere, who could help.

Between the Red Cross, local charities, churches, and friendly neighbors, people survived for a while without power. But not this time.

How many children were hungry that very minute? How many would die in the next week or month or year? She couldn't hazard a guess. In one of their down moments, Tucker had pulled up a copy of a US House of Representatives hearing almost a decade old on his phone. He'd saved it the day he received the notice of a potential solar storm.

With his solar panels charging up his electronics, he could pull up anything stored locally on his computer or phone and he was always checking to see if he could connect with the outside world. A few pages into reading the hearing transcription and it confirmed all of Madison's worst fears.

Ninety percent of the country's population would be dead within a year if an EMP destroyed the power grid. That's what the experts predicted: 90 percent. Everything was there, in black and white. Most of the 300 million people living in the United States couldn't provide for their own food or other needs.

They stopped living like that years ago.

To go back to a rural economy—one where people grew what they needed to survive instead of relying on others—they estimated the country would only support 30 million people at the most. Ten percent of the current population.

The hearing had taken place a decade a ago. The government knew and it did nothing. Nothing to shore up the power grid. Nothing to put backup generators in place or shield the grid from the effects of an EMP.

They sat by and let the country become more and more dependent on technology and further and further removed from basic subsistence living.

Madison rubbed at her eyes. Thanks to modernity, no one knew how to survive anymore. But that didn't mean some people wouldn't make it. In a year, when most had failed, there would be the survivors. The ones who adapted and overcame would still be there. Living.

She would be one of those people. So would her mom and friends and hopefully... her dad. She thought about all the times she took her family and her life for granted.

The weekends she didn't come home from college. The days she didn't hug her father before he left on an international flight. All the missed opportunities to tell them she loved them.

For so many years everyone around her only cared about the next new thing. Money. Cars. Clothes. Success.

It had all been an illusion.

Madison closed her eyes for a moment. She had to put the past behind her. Forget about the bad things and hold onto the good memories. The ones that would push her on.

Something flashed across her vision. Did I fall asleep? She blinked her eyes open. *Oh, no.*

It wasn't her nightmares of flames that caught her eye. A pair of headlights glowed in the distance.

Madison eased the shotgun strap off her shoulder and brought the gun into position. Not a single car had come this way in twenty-four hours. The chances of it being someone friendly were slim.

She eased around the side of the Nissan, crouching behind the far fender before propping her elbow up on the top for support. If they drove on by, she would stay hidden. But if they stopped…

With bated breath, she waited. The headlights grew in size, bobbing and weaving through the abandoned vehicles and debris left on the road. As the light bounced off the back of the Nissan and the top of the Jeep just beyond, the approaching car slowed.

Madison exhaled and steadied the gun.

The car eased into the parking lot, stopping twenty feet or so from the Nissan. Madison squinted into the headlights, the brightness blinding her. The engine shut off.

No one was stealing what they had left.

Madison lowered her head to catch the front sight of the gun.

CHAPTER THIRTY-ONE

WALTER

North of Sacramento, CA
6:00 a.m.

"So you're just going to go out there? You don't know if it's them."

"It's a yellow Jeep and a Nissan, Drew. It has to be them."

"What if it's not? What if it's some bad dude with a gun and you're shot before you even say a word?"

Walter rubbed his hair back and forth on the top of his head. He needed a haircut and for Drew to get off his back. "I'm telling you. My wife and daughter are in those cars."

Drew leaned toward the dashboard until the damn cat meowed on his lap. "I can't see anything inside. They've got a whole bunch of crap in the back seat."

"That's what happens when your house burns down.

You have to put everything in the car." He reached for the door handle. "I'm getting out."

"I can't drive with this shoulder. If you get shot, what the hell am I supposed to do?"

Walter ran his tongue over his lip. "Grow a pair. That might help." Before Drew could say another word, Walter pushed open the driver's side door.

He eased out and stood behind it. For all that Drew pissed him off, he had a point. The last thing he needed was his own wife shooting at him. He cupped his hands around his mouth. "Tracy! Madison!"

A voice he feared he would never hear again called out. "Kill the lights!"

"Madison, honey! It's your dad!"

"I said, kill the lights or I'll take you out."

He heard a shotgun bolt move forward. Walter's mouth fell open. Madison? His baby girl was threatening to kill him? The lights from the Jetta blinked out and Walter spun around.

Drew held up his hands. "What? You want to get shot?"

Walter exhaled and turned back around. "Madison! It's Walter, your father. Please don't shoot me."

He stood behind the door to the car, waiting. After a moment, a flashlight beam hit him square in the face. He blinked and held up his hands.

"Dad!" The light left his face and came bounding at him, bouncing all over the place. "Oh my God, Dad!"

His daughter barreled into him, practically knocking him down as she wrapped her arms around him and held tight. Walter reached out to hug her back but ended up palming the barrel of a shotgun instead.

She pulled back and smiled. Up close, he could see the tears streaking down her dirty cheeks and the happiness beneath. "You're all right."

"I am now." Walter glanced up. "Where's your mom?"

"In the car. That thing is seriously soundproof. She probably doesn't even know you're here."

"But she's okay?"

Madison nodded. "She got burned pretty bad in the fire, but it's just her hand. She's taking meds and getting better." His daughter patted his arms up and down. "What about you? Are you okay?"

"For the most part." He motioned to Drew in the passenger seat. "My co-pilot here took a bullet to the shoulder, but he'll live."

Madison ducked to look in the car and shrieked. "Fireball!" She popped back up. "Dad! You found him!" She crouched down again next to the driver's seat and the little cat stretched on Drew's lap and made his slow way over to her. Madison scooped him up and nuzzled his fur.

"Thanks for rescuing him. We thought he died in the fire."

Walter looked down at her in confusion. "When did you get a cat?"

His daughter smiled. "It's a long story." She motioned toward the Nissan. "Come on. Let's wake up Mom."

Walter exhaled. His family was alive.

He followed his daughter to the Nissan and she pulled open the passenger-side door. "Mom, wake up."

His wife jolted awake in the driver's seat. "Is something wrong? Are you okay?" She blinked hard as she focused on the cat. "Is that Fireball? Where did he come from?"

Madison smiled. "From this guy." She stepped out of the way and Walter leaned down to catch the first glimpse of his wife in way, way too long.

"Walter!" Tracy screamed and reached for the door.

As she scrambled out, Madison tugged on his arm. "Watch her left hand, okay?"

He nodded and held himself still as Tracy rushed around the back of the car to practically jump into his arms. God, it felt good to hug his wife again.

"You're alive!" She patted him all over with her one good hand just like his daughter had, tears flowing even faster than Madison's a few minutes before.

"I am. And so are you, although I heard you hurt your hand."

Tracy glanced down at her left hand and Walter's eyes followed. He sucked in a breath. Where soft, pale skin used to be, angry weeping blisters took up residence. "Are you all right?"

She nodded. "Penny gave me some old antibiotics. They're expired, but they seem to be working."

Walter exhaled in relief. "Drew needs antibiotics, too. We'll have to deal with that soon."

Tracy's brow knitted. "Who's Drew?"

Walter pointed at the Jetta. "My co-pilot from the

flight. We took off together after the crash landing. His fiancée didn't make it though, so—"

"Whoa, hold up." His wife held up her hands. "What crash landing?"

Walter laughed. "I think we have a lot to fill each other in on."

"You better believe it." Madison chimed in, still holding the little cat and smiling. "I'm going to wake everyone up, okay?"

Tracy nodded. "You do that, honey. Then we can all have some breakfast and figure out what to do next."

Walter watched his daughter walk away before turning to his wife. Slipping his arms around her waist, he pulled her close and kissed her. Her lips still fit against his so well.

Everything he'd been through the past week. Everything he did and all the sacrifices he made were worth it. He'd found his family.

Twenty years together, multiple tours of duty, the birth of his daughter and everything that followed were nothing compared to the journey ahead. Walter knew they would struggle. But together, they would survive.

He pulled back as a ragtag assortment of kids Madison's age all tumbled out of the Jeep and made their way toward the Nissan.

A teeny blonde girl who barely cleared Walter's shoulder stuck out her hand. "Brianna Clifton. I'm Madison's roommate. Well, former roommate, anyway."

Walter shook her hand before turning to a kid wearing space T-shirt with hair in desperate need of a good trim. "Tucker Eldrin. Good to meet you, sir."

The sir got him a few extra points, Walter had to admit.

Lastly, he smiled at the young man who outweighed him by a good thirty pounds and stuck out his hand. "Good to see you, Peyton."

"Good to see you, too, Mr. Sloane."

"Aren't you going to introduce me?" Drew ambled up to the lot of them, favoring his shoulder as he stopped beside Walter.

Walter smiled. "Everyone, this is Drew Jenkins. He was my co-pilot the day the grid failed. Without him, I wouldn't be standing here."

Drew shook each person's hand as the introductions went around again. "Walter has saved my life more than once in the last week. You all are lucky he's here."

"Don't we know it." Tracy smiled up at him, her big eyes brighter than the bluest ocean. "Now who's hungry? We don't have a lot to choose from, but I'm sure we can make do."

She turned to the car and began tasking each college kid with something to do. In minutes, a spread of various granola bars and bottles of water and Gatorade sat on the hood of the trunk. Each person picked out a few items and assembled in a makeshift circle in the parking lot.

Walter eased himself down between his wife and daughter and stretched out his legs. The first bite of the granola bar was the start of the best meal he'd had in years. It didn't matter that they were homeless and sitting on broken asphalt in an abandoned parking lot.

His wife sat on his left and his daughter on his right.

They were surrounded by friends, had food and water, and two working cars. What more could anyone ask for?

It might not be the future he imagined—no vacations to Italy or evenings out on the back porch with a beer and the setting sun—but it was more than he needed to survive. The power may never come back on, at least not in the way it did before, but they could still have a pretty good life.

He glanced over at Drew. As soon as breakfast ended, they would need to pack and work out a plan. Drew needed antibiotics. They all needed shelter.

But together they would work it out. After chatting and laughing and getting to know everyone, Walter finished his bottle of water and stood up. "Let's load up and get this show on the road. I hear we're off to Truckee?"

Brianna stood up, wiping off her backside as she nodded. "My parents have a cabin. More of a compound, really. There's enough room for all of us."

Walter tallied up the head count. "They have room for seven more people?"

She nodded. "And then some. As long as everyone contributes, everyone should be able to stay."

Walter nodded. Even if the Cliftons said no once they got there, leaving the big city for the mountains seemed like as good an idea as any other. "The Jetta has about a third of a tank of gas. We can load up everything that fits and try to siphon a car somewhere for more fuel. How's the Jeep?"

"It's about the same." Brianna glanced back at the

Wrangler. "We can try to rearrange and get some more stuff on the rack."

Peyton spoke up. "I'll help. It's a beast getting anything up there."

As everyone split up, each helping to prepare, Walter marveled. A week in and they had formed a makeshift little family with responsibilities and roles already determined. If this was what the future held, he had hope. He smiled and walked toward the Jetta. "Come on, Drew. Let's make some room."

CHAPTER THIRTY-TWO

TRACY

Backroads of Northern California
2:00 p.m.

Tracy stared at her husband as he drove behind Brianna's Jeep. She couldn't believe he was alive and sitting beside her. After everyone packed both cars, the kids decided it would be nice to give the Sloane family a little bit of alone time, so Tracy, Walter, and Madison piled into the Jetta and Drew squeezed in with Brianna, Tucker, and Peyton in the Jeep.

Fireball refused to leave the Jetta, so Madison snuggled with him in the back. If Tracy didn't look out the window and see the smashed-in store windows and abandoned cars, she could almost pretend the world hadn't fallen apart.

While the kids got their breakfast, Walter had filled

her in on a bit of his journey to find her, including his run-in with the National Guard. She turned to him. "Did the National Guard say anything about aid? How the government was getting along? Anything?"

Walter glanced at his daughter. "I don't think now is the best time."

"Dad. Anything you can say to Mom you can say to me. I'm an adult."

Walter frowned, but Tracy reached out and rubbed his shoulder. "Madison is right. She's faced more this last week than any nineteen-year-old should. If she can handle fleeing her college campus and getting shot at and a house fire, she can handle the truth. No matter what it is."

Tracy smiled at her daughter. Madison still looked so young, but childhood didn't linger forever. And in this new world, it was effectively over for everyone.

Her husband's hands flexed on the steering wheel. "All right. I won't sugarcoat it then. The short version is that there's no help coming. The police basically don't exist. Fire department, too. Downtown Sacramento was worse than LA in the riots. Every building burned out, every car flipped over, people shooting other people just because they can. It's chaos. Madness."

Tracy swallowed. It was worse than she expected. "What about the military?"

"Overwhelmed. The national guard is mobilized, the military too, I'd assume. When we ran into the unit from Eureka, they were headed to Sacramento to set up a defensive perimeter."

Tracy started. "From what? Do they think there's some threat? Is some other country going to take advantage of what happened?"

Walter shook his head. "No. It's not like that." He paused. "They were sealing downtown off. Locking the riot in."

Tracy's throat went dry.

"What do you mean?" Madison asked from the back seat. "How will people escape the violence?"

"They won't. Not anymore, anyway." Walter glanced at his wife, eyes full of bad memories. "We were lucky to get out. By the time we left Drew's place, the barricades were going up. If we'd stayed another hour, we might have been trapped there."

"Surely they would have let you out."

"Orders were to keep it contained. They would have shot us if they had to."

"Dad!"

"Sorry, Madison. It's the truth."

Tracy couldn't believe it. "Why didn't they send them in to stop the violence? That's what they did in the riots in '92."

"Not enough personnel. It took over ten thousand troops on the ground to get the LA riots under control and it took them days to get there. That was with electricity and the rest of the state and country at peace."

Walter shook his head. "There's no way without a means to communicate that the military can mobilize anyone in sufficient numbers. The National Guard members I spoke to didn't want to be there. A few were disappearing every day. Once they realize it's not getting better and they won't get paid for their efforts, most will leave."

"What do you mean?"

"Once those soldiers figure it out, the ones with families will leave. I spoke to a few of them. They all said the same thing: 'Why would I stay? So I can watch the end of the world while my family starves?'"

He glanced at Tracy. "In a few weeks, all that will be left of the military will be a bunch of single young men with guns, MREs, and no future to speak of. I hate to think what will happen next."

Tracy shuddered. Even after all that she'd been through, from surviving the run-in at Wanda's apartment complex to stealing a car to get back home, to the looters and the fire and everything in between, she hadn't grasped the full impact of what it all meant.

"Do you think anyone will come help us? Canada or Europe, maybe?"

Madison scoffed in the back seat. "They all hate us, Mom. I read this article right before all of this and it said movie companies have to remove all images of the American flag in their ads in order to sell their movies in Europe. Think about it. A movie poster about the Civil War or World War II where they can't show the American flag."

"Madison's right. A lot of places will cheer. The others will be afraid. Besides, we don't know they weren't affected, too." He shook his head. "Like it or not, we can't expect any help from anyone."

Tracy looked out the window. All that they had built.

Shops, restaurants, homes. Infrastructure. Technology. How many people worked for companies whose products were one hundred percent digital? The ingenuity of Americans was something to marvel.

In a half a century, the country had gone from small towns and backyard gardens to big cities with convenience stores on every corner. How many people even knew what a tomato plant looked like or could tell when a carrot was ripe and should be pulled from the ground?

Did anyone in a major city know how to hunt or raise livestock or even chop firewood and start a fire? Tracy had tried to teach Madison the basics. They backpacked, camped, and fished every summer—all the things Tracy wished she'd done as a kid.

But most families were glued to their screens, too busy typing away and snapping pictures of themselves to learn how to survive. While the world became increasingly complicated, the basics of life remained the same.

Food. Water. Shelter.

How had they forgotten that?

She tuned to her husband. "We really are on our own, aren't we?"

Walter nodded. "Yes we are."

Tracy reached out and rested her hand on top of his. "Whatever comes, we can face it together." She turned to her daughter and smiled. It wouldn't be easy, but every day that she got to wake up and see the face of her daughter and her husband would be a good day.

They might not have much, but they had each other. Together, they could survive anything. She dropped her hand and leaned back in her seat. All they needed to do was take it one day at a time.

CHAPTER THIRTY-THREE

MADISON

BACKROADS OF NORTHERN CALIFORNIA
4:00 p.m.

MADISON LEANED AGAINST THE BACK SEAT, FIREBALL soft and snuggly on her lap. She still couldn't believe her father found them. To think she almost shot him before he called out.

She laughed to herself.

"Something funny?"

"Not really." Madison leaned forward. "Hey, Mom? Can you try the radio again? We're a bit farther north. We might pick up someone."

"Madison, we've tried the radio every hour. There's no one out there."

"I know, but you could try again? Please?"

Her mother sighed and flicked on the radio,

scanning through the AM stations. A flicker of noise caught Madison's ear. "Go back. I heard something."

Her mom slowed, going lower in the stations until a voice made her freeze.

"Again, this is Mandy Patterson from Chico State. If anyone can hear me, we need help. Things are bad here. Real bad. There's five of us trapped in the radio building. We're almost out of food and water and we can't get out. The doors are locked from the outside."

Madison held her breath.

"We've tried breaking the glass, but it's got to be bulletproof or something. If we don't get out of here soon... we're all going to die. Please if you're out there, again, this is Mandy Patterson from Chico State. I'm broadcasting from the radio building on campus."

The Sloane family listened to the girl over and over until she ended the broadcast. Madison swallowed. If they tried to save her, it would mean putting them all at risk again. But if they ignored it and drove on...

"We have to help her."

"Honey, we can't." Her mom turned around in the front seat. "We've already got seven people with us. There's nowhere for any more to go. You're crammed in the back seat with bottles of water and Drew is up in the Jeep with three teenagers and enough boxed goods to make anyone claustrophobic."

"But she needs help!"

Her father spoke up. "We don't even know if it's real. How is she broadcasting? She can't do it without power. If they've got solar or wind or some backup generator, then she should be able to get out. I don't think it's worth the risk."

"Mom. Dad. Come on. What if that were me? What if I were stuck back at college begging for help? Wouldn't you want someone to save me?"

Her mom exhaled and closed her eyes. "Chico State has a hospital, right?"

Madison hesitated. "I don't know. It's smaller than a UC school, but it should have a student health center, at a minimum."

"That means current antibiotics for me and Drew."

"If there are any left." Madison's father glanced in the rear view. "This is a terrible idea. It's too risky."

Madison glanced out the window, trying to place their location. "We can't be that far from Chico. It's north of Sacramento."

Her father frowned. "I'd guess we're about thirty miles due east." He glanced at her mom. "If we're going to make a detour, we should do it now."

Her mom turned in her seat. "You really want to do this?"

Madison nodded. "Yes."

"It will put all our lives at risk."

"I know."

"Someone might die. We could risk losing all that we have."

Madison knew the danger. But she couldn't leave someone to die. Not when she was pleading for help. "I know what we're risking, but we have to try. If we don't, what kind of people are we?"

Walter eased the car to the side of the road and

honked the horn. The Jeep stopped just ahead. "Let's talk to the others. We'll put it up to a vote."

* * *

WANT TO READ MORE OF THE SLOANE FAMILY'S story? *Darkness Rises,* book three in the *After the EMP* series, is available now:

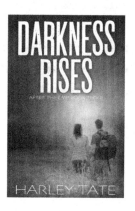

* * *

YOU CAN ALSO SUBSCRIBE TO HARLEY'S MAILING LIST for an exclusive companion short story:

www.harleytate.com/subscribe

If you were hundreds of miles from home when the world ended, how would you protect your family?

Walter started his day like any other by boarding a commercial jet, ready to fly the first leg of his international journey. Halfway to Seattle, he witnesses the unthinkable: the total loss of power as far as he can see.

Hundreds of miles from home, he'll do whatever it takes to get back to his wife and teenage daughter. Landing the plane is only the beginning.

Darkness Falls is a companion story to *After the EMP*, a post-apocalyptic thriller series following the Sloane family and their friends as they attempt to survive after a geomagnetic storm destroys the nation's power grid.

ACKNOWLEDGMENTS

A huge thanks to all of the readers of *Darkness Begins*, book one in this series! I wouldn't be continuing on with the story of the Sloane family without your support. Being able to write post-apocalyptic fiction and share it with you is the most incredible job in the world and I'm humbled by your enthusiasm!

If you have a moment, please consider leaving a review on Amazon. Every one helps new readers discover my work and helps me keep writing the stories you want to read.

Thanks again to my family for not only supporting this new endeavor, but helping fact check all those pesky little details. I couldn't have done it without you.

My goal with every book I write is to not only entertain, but also inspire the survivalist inside each of us. Being prepared isn't crazy, it's smart.

Until next time,

Harley

ABOUT HARLEY TATE

When the world as we know it falls apart, how far will you go to survive?

Harley Tate writes edge-of-your-seat post-apocalyptic fiction exploring what happens when ordinary people are faced with impossible choices.

Harley's first series, *After the EMP*, follows the Sloane family and their friends as they try to survive in a world without power. When the nation's power grid is wrecked, it doesn't take long for society to fall apart. The end of life as we know it brings out the best and worst in all of us.

The apocalypse is only the beginning.

Contact Harley directly at:

www.harleytate.com
harley@harleytate.com

Made in the USA
Monee, IL
24 February 2020